MW00415677

COMMUNIONS

Adam Lehrer

with a Postface by Nina Power

HYPERIDEAN PRESS

Copyright © 2021 by Adam Lehrer

Postface by Nina Power. Copyright © 2021.

All rights reserved. No part of this publication may be reproduced, distributed or transmitted in any form or by any means, without prior written permission.

Hyperidean Press C.I.C.
www.hyperideanpress.com

Publisher's note: This is a work of fiction. Any resemblance to real persons, entities or institutions is purely coincidental.

Udith Dematagoda and Christos Asomatos – Editors
Jamie Sunderland – Art direction and design

Communions / Adam Lehrer – First Edition September 2021

Cover: 'The Hiss of Transference' (2018) by Aleksander Hardashnakov.
Copyright © 2021.

ISBN 978-1-9163767-5-5

• foreword •

Drug addicts are the mystics of a materialist age who, no longer having the
strength to animate things and sublimate them into symbols, undertake the
inverted task of reducing them, wearing them down and eating away at them
until they reach a core of nothingness

– Le Feu Follet (1931)

These are the despondent reflections of Alain, the tragic
protagonist of Pierre Drieu La Rochelle's *Le Feu Follet*: one of
French literature's unacknowledged masterpieces. It was adapted
into a poignant film by Louis Malle in 1963, who introduced to
it one serious flaw: addiction to heroin becomes alcohol, thereby
obviating a philosophically significant element in the original.
Adam Lehrer's *Communions* approaches this subject directly, though
in my view this is only one of its main themes. *Le Feu Follet* was
inspired by Drieu's friend, the Dadaist poet Jacques Rigaut, who
had committed suicide in 1929 at a rehab clinic at the age of thirty.
Opiate addiction was then mostly the preserve of bourgeois and
upper-class bohemians. Though he produced a negligible amount
of work, Rigaut was described by his contemporaries as the most
brilliant, talented and handsome of the Dadaists. He was certainly

one of the most nihilistic. Many in the Dada movement had been brought together through a shared connection to war (either as combatants or pacifists) and a deep yearning to give some form of aesthetic articulation and sublimation to their experience.

Yet Drieu's strong identification with Riguat existed on a more unsettling plane, one marked by an obsession that had no obvious explanation. Despite their differences, Drieu seemed convinced of some fateful commonality, seeing in Rigaut's tragic and dissolute life, and within the fragmentary and unrealized work left behind - something of his own future. Drieu had distinguished himself in the First World War by leading a bayonet charge on a machine gun positon at the Battle of Charleroi. In common with many of his generation, he was a man who couldn't seem to get out of the trenches - long after the actual war had ended. In 1945, Drieu La Rochelle would also to take his own life upon the liberation of France. He would die a traitor, a fascist collaborator with the Vichy Regime and the Nazi occupation - leaving behind a compelling body of work that will forever be tainted by his actions.

At the beginning of Joseph Conrad's *Lord Jim*, those who witness the trial of the eponymous hero's moment of cowardice and desertion are incredulous because he seemed to all appearances 'one of us' - a man of the sea, bound to a sacred fraternity through shared experience, and thus privy to certain moral codes and metaphysical imperatives. Jim eventually finds redemption only at the expense of his life: the price one apparently must pay for spiritual betrayal. We can see that the bond of experience was even in Conrad's time a necessarily aesthetic one. Having spent the majority of my adult life convinced that I entirely lack the credulous gene, I do occasionally find myself incapable of disavowing an uncanny contiguousness of experience shared with some of the people I've encountered. Though I have never met Adam Lehrer in person, we're of similar age and had a comparable musical and cultural *bildung*. As it happens, when he was approaching the grim apogee of his addiction in the summer of 2013, we were living only a block from one another in Bushwick. Although we apparently went to the same bars, gigs and clubs – and perhaps even crossed paths – we never became acquainted until last year. I had gone to New York to consult the archives at the NYPL, but spent the majority of my time either blackout drunk or hungover in the sweltering heat without an air-conditioner. I was also grappling with what was, in retrospect, a debilitating addiction to Xanax, which I had originally been prescribed for a severe panic disorder by an otherwise indifferent doctor.

Commonality of experience, though unquestionably rooted in narcissistic identification, has of late become a potent form of solidarity, all the more intense for being mediated through technologies that continuously render our perception of reality aesthetic. This has had many consequences in the past decade, most of them unwelcome. In the first instance, it has led to the proliferation of online communities and identities constituted solely on the basis of shared experiences, to which many pledge an intense fealty. But the constitution of the ego is a perilous and deceptive enterprise, and one necessarily based on misrecognition. We are now forced into a quotidian confrontation with this misrecognition, and the results are unsurprisingly pathological. On the one hand, we are compelled to project an idealized, stable and contained self onto the world for the purposes of validation and recognition by a symbolic order, which then permits us to take our place within the various aforementioned 'communities' of experience. At the same time, however, we must face the fundamental inauthenticity that is at the heart of the ego – the prospect that this idealized self (in appearance, word and deed) is nothing but a fraudulent version of our true self, which bears little resemblance to the projection. Are these experiences in fact our own, or ones we have acquired vicariously, deceptively, or through mimesis? This was a disjunction that previous generations likely never had to confront with such obscene regularity, and one that is driving people to newer and higher levels of hysteria. The bonds of experience are mired in unreality and self-deception, but are horribly tangible nonetheless.

Nowhere is this more apparent than in popular criticism of art, music, literature and culture. I write with little malice when I observe that such criticism has become entirely servile and mediocre in recent years. It is now seemingly practiced only by writers who share a tedious and over-wrought lexicon, but have remarkably little to say aside from how a work speaks to their own subjectivity. The uniformity of such criticism becomes clear when we consider that its pretentious style can be seamlessly applied to any cultural product with little modification. This is mostly due to the complicity of the corporate media and publishing worlds, which exert a hegemonic influence and clearly prefer frictionless and banal cultural outputs that revel in aesthetic mediocrity. The functionaries of these entities serve the interests of a reader who they erroneously imagine to be no different from themselves; one who prefers tepid bourgeois morality and facile appeals to the affective politics of 'representation' (a corollary of identification) over actual artistic merit. Lehrer, having practiced as a critic under such constraints, has seemingly come to a realization uncommon among his contemporaries; that it is now necessary to drop all pretense in order to force a confrontation that can no longer be deferred: what is the meaning and purpose of such criticism? Here he writes about (and through) the work of others, but there is absolutely no question that he is writing about himself; his tastes, his obsessions and his experiences. It is an attempt at exorcism, but one open to the possibility of complete possession.

Communions thus confronts the ghostly remainder of the bonds of experience, real and imaginary (increasingly the same thing) and their unwieldy influence on criticism and contemporary culture. He does so with a degree of honesty not apparent in similar creative endeavors, which often end up producing what is too generously referred to as *auto-fiction*, but should more accurately be called *ego-fiction*. The questions I view as implicit in this work are essential ones for the present moment: what is the value (if any) of the identification derived from shared experience? Is it merely an affective and sentimental attachment too readily exploited and recuperated by a technological Total State comprised of vast, borderless, semio-corporations? Or can this bond of shared experience, at its core an aesthetic and spiritual one, portend something greater than the sum of these forces...and even point to a way beyond them.

Udith Dematagoda, Shinjuku, Tokyo, 2021

For the artists and the fiends, living and dead.

Dedicated to MT and BB

CONTENTS

CHAPTER 1
◆ parasites ◆

This is a book about addiction, and the hyper-specific character of opiate addiction in particular. This is a book about the *artist as addict*, and the type of art that is produced by the opiate addicted artist. Addiction is often reduced to a series of highs and lows; wellness and sickness; euphoria and despair. While this comes close to describing the experience of an opiate addict, what it fails to adequately communicate is that a haunting singularity courses through a long term, committed addiction, even as it flits between these polarities. It's all one form of the same character.

What is that character? This is the aspect of addiction that is hardest to explain. Is it the gnawing phantom the addict finds himself living with throughout the latest stages of his use? Whether broke, sick, desperately moving around the city in search of a score, or high as a kite, painless, and nodding out to The Velvet Underground in your apartment - the specter forever looms. Is it Guilt? Guilt and addiction are inextricably linked. The need for the opiate pushes you in directions, from petty crimes to atrocious acts against the people you love, unthinkable in a state of sobriety. Guilt, however is almost always overpowered by the force of addiction. Is it depression? Lots of addicts are depressed, but most aren't clinically so; they're just uncomfortable in their own skin. The specter of addiction is all of these things and more. The essence of addiction is an intensified experience of the material world. When you are constantly in need of one specific chemical to put yourself at ease, you become hyper-aware of the obstacles presented by the material world: money, transportation, interpersonal dynamics, danger, and the body itself. Opiate addiction is a shockingly corporeal state of being. You will never be made more aware of the knicks and knacks in your body, the grotesqueries of your digestive tract, the fragility of your veins, flesh and blood, and the brutality of your central nervous system than when you are addicted. With awareness of the body, comes an awareness of the environment. This is the state of addiction: heightened physical, mental, and spiritual awareness. The effects of dope don't dilute this knowledge: even under the euphoria, it haunts you.

William S. Burroughs was the writer who best manifested the singular feeling of life in addiction. Burroughs's writing isn't about addiction, it is addiction. To read Burroughs is to be offered a glimpse into addiction itself, which can be both thrilling and disturbing. While known for its transgressive quality, the true aim of Burroughs's writing is to make you feel what an addict feels. Not just to see what an addict experiences, but to live inside their pitiable skin; to feel the burn of sickness and the warm itch of the high. Burroughs wants you to understand a life buried under addiction and what it means to replace all the desires and needs of the world with just one, all powerful, all encompassing, all corrosive hunger. He wants you to comprehend addiction as a modern condition. Burroughs is the artist of addiction, its greatest manifesting agent.

The addict's memory is a fixed entity locked in stasis. Addiction tends to construct a temporal wall around experience. When I look back on my days as a daily user of junk, OxyContin, Morphine, and all other manner of narcotic pills and powders I could get my hands on, I cannot recall linear sequences of events in the way I can mentally reconstruct my childhood, or the memory of a city I used to inhabit. Looking back upon the life of an addict, after years of sobriety, all that remains is the feeling of living in a cycle under which all time collapses. During the months or years the addict spends in the throes of junk, memory folds in on itself as a fixed space. All of these experiences and recollections liquefy until it begins to feel like an episode in my life that never actually happened. And yet, at the same time, like the only part of my life that has ever actually happened. No other artist captures this internal contradiction better than Burroughs. In his writing, addiction pulverizes time and absorbs its events into one amorphous whole.

Burroughs developed such insight due to the sheer length of his use. The height of his addiction lasted a monstrous 15 years, yet his attitude towards this legacy in later years makes one wonder if he ever stopped at all. Most addicts hit bottom after only about five years: Burroughs managed to triple that. As the Harvard-educated son of a well-to-do Kentucky family, Burroughs maintained a splendid level of health throughout his long addiction. Remove his access to resources and he succumbs to death or serious illness way before he can even begin to understand the essence of addiction (opioid related health problems are much more common among poor people who can't maintain a healthy supply and are thus often forced into crime and other lifestyles to support the habit). It is not the intensity but the duration that breaks the will to resist. In Burroughs's case, his provenance in a world of privilege is what afforded him his specific artistic viewpoint, as the gateway between American prosperity and its injuriously malevolent underbelly.

Burroughs did not merely capture the aesthetic of this contradiction in the abstract. Rather, he possessed a set of disciplined techniques pioneered to create a literature that destabilized the experience of time. In a sense, addiction is a repudiation of the determinism imposed by temporality. By the very nature of Burroughs's subject matter, the artist knew that he must find a way to emphasize the bizarre sense of time and memory experienced by the addict. This would prove fundamental to transposing the *feeling* of opiate addiction onto prose. Burroughs was no Marxist ("I don't want to hear about the masses and I never fucking did."). He had absolutely no intention to disrupt the temporal path of the novel. The singular aesthetic preoccupation of his work − *addiction* − is a mode that naturally disrupts linearity independent of ideology; a materialism which does not pretend to political aims.

Burroughs was constantly looking for ways to give a definable form to the uncanny temporal singularity of addiction, and in the process he opened up the craft of writing to techniques originating in the visual arts. Burroughs had little respect for the medium of photography as a viable artistic form but made great use of it as a strategy for complicating time and memory. He would photograph everything: friends, lovers, or buildings that he had some kind of primal urge to destroy. He would then re-photograph the images over and over, creating mosaics and collages. In the process, he destroyed the linear and folded it over into a circular loop, a visual interpretation of how the addict experiences life. The cycle, the repetition, the man reduced to mechanical force animated by one all-powerful need. Now that he could *see* addiction, Burroughs was able to start

18

rendering this particular sequencing of life textually. But to do that, he would also have to recreate this technique with language.

Cut. Burroughs was already convinced that Brion Gysin was one of the greatest painters he had come across. Any narrative or any passage, say, of poetic images is subject to any number of variations all of which may be valid in their own right. Psychic landscape of his own. Language is a virus from outer space. Surrealists in Paris 1934. Dadaism. Expelled by André Breton. But to what end? Gysin. Any narrative or any passage, say, of poetic images is subject to any number of variations all of which may be valid in their own right. Up. Brion. Besides its function in the formal problematization of meaning I'm more interested in how the cut-up addresses the problem of the addict's experience of temporality. *Language is a virus from outer space.*

Naked Lunch is less a coherent story than an assortment of fragmented vignettes. It can be read in any order. I happen to own a reprint which places what was initially its opening paragraph – in which Burroughs' literary alter-ego, the junk addicted agent William Lee, murders two beat cops and flees while simultaneously in search of junk to make sure his supply is fat while he's on the lamb - at the tail end of the novel. It works every bit as well. *Naked Lunch* is structured to be read out of order. It is structured to manifest the temporal loop experienced by the addict. A blur of events that weave in and out of one another, tethered solely by the omnipresent need of addiction itself. Addiction is the glue. It is not the intensity but the duration that breaks the will to resist. Extrapolating from addiction, Burroughs arrived at an "Algebra of Need" which governs all aspects of modern life. Even absent junk, this need is replaced by other addictions and dependencies. In *Naked Lunch*, the addict can stand witness to the atrocities of a

19

totalitarian regime. The addict can stand witness to the deranged and macabre medical procedures of a sadist doctor. But the addict will not experience these occurrences as a straight line. They will be folded into a functionally indistinguishable circular experience.

Time is meaningless to the addict. Similarly, Burroughs's *Nova Trilogy* directly incorporates the cut-up method in writing. These are arguably his most formally radical experiments. Reading these novels is like plunging through a bewildering fog where everything that happens is imbued with the vaguest unreality. If *Naked Lunch* was the height of the junkie's still functioning addiction, the *Nova Trilogy* is rock bottom. Everything that happens lacks any sequential structure. Every occurrence is blurred out of focus as addiction seeps into every pore of the senses. Burroughs's writing, slicing and folding in of words, paints the confusing portrait of an addict, totally lost in need, severed from time itself.

Smile of idiot death spasms – slow vegetable decay filmed his amber flesh – always there when the egg cracks and the white juice spurts from ruptured spines – from his mouth floated coal gas and violets – The boy dropped his rusty black pants…

In this text from *The Soft Machine*, Burroughs's cut-up parallels the late-stage addict's burnt-out senses. Nothing holds any narrative sequential cohesion. The addict barely registers what's happening around him, everything is turned to visual fragments and haphazard incidents. Nothing else matters. Many artists experimented with techniques and creative strategies, but Burroughs always had specific goals in mind. Perception in opioid addiction is exceedingly difficult to render onto page, but with these pseudo-surrealist fragments, Burroughs narrates the collapse of the human psyche barely glued together by the burning sensation of need.

"Junk narrows consciousness", Burroughs told an interviewer in 1967. The opiate for him was a painkiller that lessens the perception of reality. It has no transcendental qualities. It is of no consequence to the cosmos, the universe, or that which lies beyond. On the contrary, to use opiates is to completely disconnect yourself from any spiritual dimension. To use junk is to be brought down to the level of pure base matter; it allows you to feel at one with the dying flesh you inhabit. Burroughs is the artist of opiate addiction, not of its transcendental highs. Junk made Burroughs an observant writer for the same reason it made him a talented, cunning, and efficient shadow agent of the CIA. Without it, he tended to disconnect from reality all together. With junk, however, he channeled his mystic energy into his body and into his physical surroundings. Junk made him one with reality, allowing him to render it to the page, but also to inform his insidious handlers in intelligence. *Language is a virus from outer space.*

Burroughs was convinced that there was no such thing as an accident, and he often thought himself driven by a "malevolent force." Dark magic flowed through Burroughs. Gysin called it his "Ugly Spirit." While junk seemed to repress the Ugly Spirit, without junk Burroughs succumbed to it. Alcohol made the Ugly Spirit a force of chaos and unpredictability. Its power over Burroughs resulted in the accidental murder of his wife Joan Vollmer.

I am forced to the appalling conclusion that I would never have become a writer but for Joan's death, and to a realization of the extent to which this event has motivated and formulated my writing. I live with the constant threat of possession, a constant need to escape from possession, from Control.

Without this chain of events, Burroughs would have never become the artist he became, and we would not be able to look to him now. He needed junk to anchor himself to the debased reality of day-to-day existence. Burroughs believed that men of reason were wrong. And yet he needed to think like one. He was aware that opiate addiction produces states opposed to transcendence. It brings life to an utterly material understanding of economic and social relations. This is the core of addiction in Burroughs and therein lies its distinctly modern character...

The orgasm has no function in the junk

The nature of libido is fundamental to understanding Burroughs' conception of addiction as an undeniably corporeal state. *I am a ghost wanting what every ghost wants-a body-after the Long Time moving through odorless alleys of space where no life is.* Sexuality is material, of course, but desire is of a partly metaphysical character. Countless mystic belief systems embedded sexuality into their rituals and codes. The Celtic Druids believed that through harnessing sexual energy, man could exert transcendental will over their environment. The *Ordo Templi Orientis*, the occult organization founded by Theodor Reuss and later headed by Aleister Crowley, associated certain sexual acts with the climbing of a ladder; the more lewd the act (masturbatory, vaginal, anal) was, the closer the occultist grew to the "Hermit Triad." The practitioners of "Chaos Magick" – pioneered by the likes of occult novelist Peter J. Carroll and Throbbing Gristle's Genesis P-Orridge in the 1970s – attempted to wed the occult practices of English artist Austin Osman Spare to arrive at what they called the "Gnostic State." *Language is a virus from outer space.* Reaching this state required intense sexual arousal.

Burroughs's characters encounter an onslaught of vicious sexual crimes and stomach-churning acts of depravity with mute resignation and indifference. Because their desires have been subsumed by the need for junk, they are no longer able to attach a moral or spiritual dimension to these crimes and to react with the indignity one would normally exhibit in the face of such libidinal cruelty. It has always been interesting that Burroughs, in addition to being the author of junk, is also known as an author of homosexuality. Yet all sexuality in Burroughs is devoid of erotic character, reduced to mere pornography. *Language is a virus from outer space.* There is nothing in his work resembling authentic desire. Because desire in Burroughs is not autonomous. Perhaps not too ironically, the detachment of Burroughs's characters isn't dissimilar from what he displayed in his own personality. Burroughs fucked for the sheer act of fucking. Aside from Gysin, there's little evidence that he connected to anyone in a deep spiritual way. He just needed to fuck, from time to time, the way that we need to fix. He'd grow infatuated but lose interest quickly – as was the case with his obsession with Ginsberg. He often found himself drawn to heterosexual men, often young and mentally weak, who he'd coax into sex through feigned vulnerability or promises of lewd adventure. He was a sneaky bastard, mischievous to the core; in his sexual relations we are offered a glimpse into those malicious qualities that Burroughs believed would make him an excellent intelligence agent. In 1952, Burroughs's biography becomes somewhat patchy – by some accounts he moved to Bernalillo, a town outside of Albuquerque, New Mexico and lived there for a number of months. In 2006, a shallow grave containing the remains of three men were found. The men were Mexican agricultural laborers, thought to be working as male prostitutes but not seen since the 1950s. *Language is a virus from outer space.*

It's hard to know whether Burroughs was already deep in junk at that point, but it would make sense. To be in the throes of junk is to be utterly tethered to the material world. Addiction to opiates is to be free of transcendental thought. We are all locked in systems. But opiate addiction makes the addict hyper aware of the set of the material relations we inhabit. This is equally burdensome and freeing; Burroughs understood that better than any artist that dealt with the subject. To be free of libido is to be free of the forces of control and desire. The junkie's separation with the spiritual in any sense is reflected in Burroughs's characters' indifference to the cruelty surrounding them. They see the world through what Burroughs describes as "the canceled eyes of junk". William Lee's tacit acceptance of Dr. Benway's sadistic methods of population control is the junkie's relationship to power. It is what it is. Dr. Benway prefers "prolonged mistreatment" of a population over direct torture, which he finds inefficient. "'Many subjects are vulnerable to sexual humiliation," Benway confides. "'Nakedness, simulation with aphrodisiacs, constant supervision, constant supervision to embarrass the subject and prevent release of masturbation." Lee, Burroughs's literary persona, sees the ills in Benway's methods but does not act. This is the state of opiate addiction. The addict is hyperaware of the matrixes of violence that define power, yet absent libidinal energy, cannot confront them. The addict merely acknowledges the existence of systematic oppression while embracing addiction as its compressed form.

To be addicted, Burroughs understood, is to be deeply modern. Had Burroughs not experienced his 15 years of addiction, he would have never been able to live in this world. His own inclinations were that of a mystic, and indeed allowed him to develop fascinating insights into addiction. Opioid addiction is a heightened sense

24

of the contemporary world, its codes and its patterns. Addiction is a metaphor for the modern condition in Burroughs, but it also *is* the modern condition in Burroughs. Without addiction, Burroughs would have floated above reality in the clouds with the mystics. Junk brought him back down to earth among the vermin. Lost in the sickness. There is no magic in addiction. There is need. And with need comes alienation. And alienation moves you through the city. Addiction is a state of extreme presence.

Burroughs believed that in the 20th century, power took on new characteristics. It became a gaseous force that seeps into your blood streams, plants itself into the brain, and lives inside you as a parasite. The parasite makes your decisions for you as it takes control. In liberalism, one can only be free in the market of desire. And desire is not an expression of autonomous agency. Desire is drilled into you, mainlined into your bloodstream via politics, advertising, school, and all the apparatuses that together form Western bourgeois society. In late capitalism, desire is a parasite. Burroughs was, as stated previously, a mystic and a romanticist. But the 20th century, and the shift from industrial to late capitalism collapsed every such notion. Burroughs' addiction was fundamental to his ability to observe these cultural shifts. Addiction is one of the fundamental states of being in the contemporary world, and because Burroughs used addiction to these ends, he best interpreted it as such. Burroughs had a natural aversion to politics and ideology. He couldn't separate activism from the systems that it claimed to oppose, because activism and ideology are all in service of the same hegemony.

In Burroughs's work, addiction functions as an embodiment of an imposed, artificial desire, a form of a Spinozist "alien occupying force." *I am a ghost wanting what every ghost wants-a body-after the Long*

25

Time moving through odorless alleys of space where no life is. Burroughs believed that there was no authentic desire in modern society; everything was manufactured and enforced. Burroughs practiced psychoanalysis on a young Ginsberg. Ginsberg's most terrifying self-revelations revolved around his fears that nobody loved him. Burroughs found Ginsberg's anxieties to be banal: "Why do you need someone to love you?" For Burroughs, love was merely another alien occupying force. This observation is at the heart of what makes Burroughs explorations of addiction so rich compared to others who dealt with the subject. His addiction isn't just a form of human degradation; it's also a bizarre form of liberation. To be overtaken by the alien occupying force of opiate addiction is to be freed from the countless other tedious constraints of modernity.

Given certain known factors in an equation and the equation comprising a situation of absolute need — any form of need — you can predict the results. Leave a sick junkie in the back room of a drugstore and only one result is possible. The same is true of anyone in a state of absolute hunger, absolute fear, etc. The more absolute the need, the more predictable the behavior becomes until it is mathematically certain.

A society whose survival is continuously in contention becomes all too easy to control. *It is not the intensity but the duration of pain that breaks the will to resist.* Burroughs imagined the cut-up as a metaphor for the ways that power in the Information Age was rewriting human code, turning us into machines of desire all too easy to regulate, control and manipulate. Burroughs's artistic rendering of addiction paints a dark parallel to the evolution of power during the collapse of early 20th century institutions and the ascent of neoliberalism as governing orthodoxy in the 1970s.

In *Nova Express*, the final novel of the trilogy, Burroughs applies the cut-up method to a narrative that hues towards speculative fiction. *Nova Express* best realizes Burroughs's conception of the addict as host and parasite. The book chronicles the battle of wills between the Nova Mob and the Nova Police. The Nova Mob are viruses of desire, Burroughs' metaphor for culture, which he believes to be the most insidious agent of Control. The Nova Police focus on addicts, homosexuals, dissidents, and criminals. They are of an older, more direct, and less all-encompassing form of control.

The technical advances which enabled recording, fragmenting, and cutting up translate into expansive technologies of control. Now the masses can be mechanically turned against one another. Burroughs saw all of this. And it's unclear whether he would have seen any of it had he not become aware of it as an addict. The addict feels the alien occupying forces of control as a physical sickness, which affords (or punishes) one with an acute awareness of unfreedom. The parasite will always get inside.

The following pages should be read as a case study of the character of addiction, told through the perspectives of artists afflicted with the parasite of addiction. I am not interested in the idea that opiates stimulate the neural centers of creativity. I am not interested in that because it is a lie. I am interested in addiction in the way that Burroughs understood it. I will look to the opiate addicted artist not as an enlightened mystic, but instead as an artist who is deeply aware of the contradictions and systems of control that they inhabit. The life of the addict – to be driven by a need that manifests as a sickness – is to become all too aware of the recurring nature of existence. Burroughs knew that there was no such thing as freedom. *Language is a virus from outer space.* He understood that all our desires are parasites that we have no power to oppose. He knew this because he colluded with the intelligence services that dictated the terms of the reality that the drugs kept him grounded within. He knew this because of the secret knowledge that his status as an intelligence asset afforded him. And, he knew this, because he was addicted to opiates, the most potent and recognizable of parasites. The parasite that latches onto you, drags you down, and constantly reminds you that you have a body that is tethered to a physical environment shaped by control systems and matrices of power. The irony of the opiate addict is that although the narcotic creates a buffer between themselves and the reality around them – a warm, protective layer – the actual structure of addicted life is one which makes the subject hyperaware of their imprisonment in a specific array of social relations.

◆ last day ◆

Dash woke up at noon on July 13, 2009. He'd only checked into the hotel earlier that morning, moving in with a boombox, tapes, books, and clothes all cluttered into a few bags of luggage. It was the first day of his planned three day stay. The decade that made him an unbearable cliché of wealth and fame was nearly over. It was too much to think about; better not think about it at all. Dash remembered when he was younger, waking up on the floor in cramped, studio apartments, surrounded by alcoholic graffiti artists, skateboarders and musicians, sweating profusely. His living conditions were disgusting, and to escape them he had to cultivate his ambition.

He felt like he didn't need to sleep. Life was wide open. "Keep moving, avoid the heat." Avoid self-reflection. There were always more drugs down the block. There was always another petty transgression, an opportunity for exuberance. There was always more *life*, waiting to be seized. But here, in this expensive, rustic themed downtown hotel, he was utterly comfortable, luxuriating in the air conditioning. And he didn't want to get up. He didn't need to. Everything he could have possibly wanted was right here in this hotel room. An ounce of heroin. Three and a half grams of cocaine. Beer. Vodka. Some ketamine that Hanna left and said he could keep. He had his records, his books, his magazines, his tapes. He didn't want to make art anymore. He didn't want to go anywhere. He should just leave the city, but he was too comfortable.

The room stank of tobacco, butane, and stale vodka. Dash, who had the silk linens tucked under his neck as he kept his eyes closed, drifting in and out of a full state of consciousness, was lost in the memories of the last decade. It was as if adulthood had never truly presented itself to him. Instead, it grew in him like a parasite. It was like junk that way. Deep down, you know it's going to get bad. But you play along, as you enjoy the first few experiences. Then they get heavier and more frequent. Next thing you know, you're a junkie. Or, an adult. You always knew it'd get to this, but you couldn't stop it. It's fucked up, man. Dash felt an uncomfortable itch on his cock; lifting the sheets up, he noticed the red rings of raw flesh. It was only five hours ago that he'd attempted masturbation, desperate for a hard-on that never came. He used to be able to perform sexually on any number of drugs. This impotence was new.

His eyes were now finally open. He cracked his neck and stretched his shoulders backwards. Dash suddenly felt dread about his coming birthday. On July 27, he'd be 28. He was still, in most people's eyes, a kid. He had his whole life before him. That's what most people say about someone as rich and famous as him. But he was tired of playing the role imposed on him. "Fucking vultures," he thought to himself. He got out of bed and reached into the drawer of his nightstand to grab a spike that was still sharp enough to not leave a track mark.

Dash felt much more comfortable in a sprawl. He didn't like dirtiness, but he liked stuff. He loved calling heroin "junk," because that word allowed him to make sense of his dedication to the drug. He felt most comfortable while surrounded by detritus and clutter. In a sense, this was an extension of his practice – disparate, chaotic and obscure.

He hated how critics wrote about his work. They only talked about drugs and blowjobs, but never understood the way that his work essentially functioned. He turned spaces into large-scale assemblages. He turned everything around him - old pornography, empty packs of cigarettes, used drug baggies, pulp fiction novels - into him. If there was art here at all, Dash thought, it was more innovative than anyone had ever given him credit for. His predilection towards salacious controversy was an act of self-invention crucial for any artist. It was why he adored Huncke and Lou Reed. His persona overshadowed the formal aspects of his art. He was a lousy painter, but he interacted with the world in a way that was unique, a method of engagement that was all his own. He felt disgust at his role in all this. He tried to push it out of his mind.

As was his morning ritual, Dash walked over to the pile of tapes, CDs and records lying in the corner of the room opposite his bed. He dumped everything on the floor after checking in and must have passed out shortly after. He'd recently become interested in harsh noise music, since it felt closer to the kind of creative subculture that he fetishized and tried to embody despite being, let's face it, a commercial sell out visual artist making millions of dollars. He thumbed through tapes by Skin Crime, Filthy Turd, Black Leather Jesus and The Rita, and tried to remember if he liked any of them. He had no clue what they sounded like, really. They looked good stacked on the living room floors, though. He set the boombox to the side of the antique marble hearth, connecting it to a nearby outlet. Giving up on feeling adventurous, he grabbed a tape of *Exile on Main St.* and skipped to track 8. "Sweet Black

Angel." Someone had told him recently that the song was about Angela Davis, which Dash thought was kind of lame. He believed that artists as great as Mick Jagger and Keith Richards should exist beyond politics. That great art should be libidinal, like energy flowing outwards and inwards. It works like a drug; once it takes effect, reality melts away. But either way, it's a great fucking song.

Got a sweet black angel…
Got a pin-up girl…

Dash nodded his head up and down and closed his eyes as he sat cross-legged on the floor. Still naked, save for a pair of black Calvin Klein boxer shorts, he pulled the coffee table towards him, and grabbed three bags of junk (his regular morning fix). He gently released three bags onto a bent spoon, extracted water from a battle of *Dasani*, and squirted it carefully back onto the spoon, the dope dissolving into it. The crackle of the cooking heroin still made his heart pound. There were dollops of sweat on his neck and around his eyelids. He was low level sick – sweaty, achy and anxious – but hadn't had serious withdrawal symptoms since 2006. Ever since he was named a "23-year old Master", he'd never been without a large quantity of drugs. When he tried weaning his way off heroin with the use of Suboxone, he timed his relapse perfectly. At exactly 48 hours after putting the film of chemicals underneath his tongue, he blasted six bags of heroin up his arm, overpowering whatever was left of the opioid blockers.

Dash wrapped his favorite leather belt, the one with the coiled snake for a buckle, around his arm. He pushed the needle in without hesitation, extracted his blood to let it mix with the dope, and shot it back into his vein. His head fell back for a moment, and he was warm again. He got back up. And walked over to the machine to make coffee. "Happy" was now playing through the boombox speaker.

Dash dug through his pile of clothes until he found his favorite pair of black jeans and a Samhain t-shirt. He caught his reflection in the mirror. He didn't even look like a human being. "Why did this happen?" he thought to himself, staring directly into his pinned pupils and then up and down the reflection of his body. Somewhere along the line, he was reduced to a living Terry Richardson photograph. He didn't look real to himself, almost like "Dash Snow" was nothing but an affectation that he at some point had adopted. It was embarrassing, the degree to which he let fantasy and MTV "outsiderdom" shape his own personality. Was it all his fault? Definitely partly, he thought. Sitting down at the coffee table, he couldn't shake the feeling of shame. It grows like a parasite. Drugs could only suppress it, never rid his system of it entirely.

Dash grabbed a pack of Marlboro Reds from his bathroom counter after taking a piss and fired one up as he sat down to drink his coffee. His egocentrism, which was honestly a new development within his psyche - like a vulgar byproduct of seven years of flattery by the famous and powerful - had become his constant companion. Adulation and addiction force the psyche inwards, making it narcissistic. Dash took a sip of coffee and picked one of the three loose cigarettes out of the pack. Lighting it, he inhaled for several moments. "I'm depressed," he realized.

He had friends who suffered from this affliction, but he always approached life wide open. As long as he kept moving, his mind was clear. No more. He was cloudy and bothered. His drug use had always been severe, but it had taken a darker turn in recent months. For the first time he felt like heroin was severing him off from the world rather than allowing him to bond with it. He thought about all the times he played up "the rebel." He'd tell interviewers that he didn't believe in laws or systems. To an extent, he still felt that way. And yet, the system's modes of belief had seeped into his self-conception. He no longer was able to see himself from within, he only saw what everyone else saw. He'd internalized the exterior world's insistence on who Dash Snow is. When he looked in the reflection of his mirror, he saw a parody. Dash finished the cigarette and hacked a loogie into the trash can. It was almost 2 PM. He had been awake for two hours. He'd waited long enough. No more inhibitions for today.

Dash grabbed three more packets of heroin – each emblazoned with a red Adidas logo – and prepared another shot. In terrible need of a jolt of uplift, he tapped his finger into a bag of cocaine, emptying about a quarter of a gram onto the spoon. When he tied off, the warmth of the dope high was saturated with an energetic burst and a bodily numbness. Bored and buzzing, Dash walked back over to his collection of stuff to thumb through books and magazines. He first grabbed a stack of old copies of the *NY Post* that he was using as an image source for his future projects. Dash couldn't read words when he was on speedballs. He could look at them but they didn't register. He went back to his music collection, avoiding the answering machines, knowing Jade's voice would be on one of them, asking if he was all right. He wanted some time alone. Dash liked being elusive. It was often joked that to find him at all, one would first have to find his friends Ryan and Dan. But Dash hadn't even spoken with them recently. He used to think that what didn't kill him would just make him stronger, but already now needing another cocaine fix (he snorted two more lines off a CD case while thinking this), he realized that what hadn't yet killed him was only making him lamer. More pathetic. The biggest cliché in a city run on them. He put on Neil Young's "Walk On."

Dash started to think about Jade and his daughter. He'd already blown one marriage (Agathe wasn't speaking with him these days). The weirdest part about fatherhood was that there was no unique feeling about it. It just meant that everything you used to do without thinking - crimes, reckless sex, drugs - you now thought about twice. Dash snorted another line of cocaine and flipped a baggy of heroin beneath his thumbs and lit another cigarette. He thought about New York, and the new millennium. Everything new was old, tired, possibly dead. It wasn't supposed to be like this. In his pile of books, he found a text on Henry Darger: *In the Realms of the Unreal.* After tying off another two bags, Dash lay down on his back on the floor, perching his head on a pillow, and flipped through the book. The drawings had a totally hypnotic effect. Cute little girls in vulgar, bright colors, frolicking naked in idyllic nature, hanging dead in ritualized spectacles... Everything Darger dared not show anyone, all the anxiety, curiosity, sexuality, perversion and innocence was in these drawings. Dash envied him.

He wondered if his life and career would have gone differently in other eras. Maybe, Dash thought, if he'd been an artist 20 or 30 years ago – making work similar to that he was making now – he could have spent his life actually at the fringes. Maybe he could have killed himself before ever being discovered. Maybe, like Darger, some mortuary crew could just find a pile of his collages and polaroids lying next to Dash's decaying corpse, the smell of the rot seeping into his artistic materials. Maybe he could have been an outsider artist who lived a life in obscurity to be recognized in death.

Dash thought maybe he was supposed to be one of those authentic, degenerate criminal artists. But after MTV, after Osama Bin Laden, authenticity became the easiest thing to brand. "This guy is so real," Dash imagined a fictional editor at a fictional failing magazine, "He does heroin and likes guns, put him on the cover now!"

"I never had a fucking shot," he muttered out loud, exhaling the smoke, pinching the pit of his stomach detecting a queasiness rising to the surface. Dash would always be "Dash Snow," the art world's favorite junkie and little more than a sales pitch for the repugnant people he hated. He'd give up every dollar he'd made to experience something real - anything - that was real. Or so he thought.

Dash was exceptionally adept at pretending he was teflon. It was easy for him to play the "junkie rebel" card and feign apathy concerning artworld affairs. He never even considered calling himself an artist until Ryan told him that there might be something to his Polaroids, and artworld collector queens were probably jerking off to the pictures of him in *The Kids Are All Right*. So, to an extent, Dash didn't care about what they said about him because he didn't care at all. He snorted three more bumps of cocaine off the edge of his pocket-knife and buzzed back over to the tapes and the boombox. Feeling romantically melancholic, he put on Leonard Cohen's *I'm Your Man*.

If you want a lover
I'll do anything you ask to

Dash loved to be hated. Cooking up another shot, he remembered a review from *Frieze*. He picked a piece of text from it that he'd cut out of the magazine and pathetically kept in his wallet like a trophy to his own apathy (which was actually a cover for his deep insecurity).

From the relentless blogs debating how often he speaks to his wealthy De Menil family to a recent New York magazine article profiling his delinquency, drug use and graffiti crew, Snow's image and his antics garner far more column inches than his art.

"Fuck you, cunt" thought Dash, blood dripping from the injection site. He lifted his arm to his mouth and licked it clean like a feral animal.

Against his will, Dash found himself pining for more acclaim. Dan and Ryan were already making that leap, but Dash's background and reputation prevented him from getting there. Though he'd never admit it, Dash knew he had an authenticity that would remain out of reach for his friends. This lifestyle, the criminal lifestyle, was one that they were only experimenting with. But for Dash, this was his natural state. Dash scraped together some heroin and cocaine together into a bump on the coffee table, and sniffed it hard up his nose, gagging on the drip. Maybe this is why Dan and Ryan were already becoming artworld darlings: they knew how to package this lifestyle into an artistic brand. They were art school kids slumming it - even during those times when they were smoking PCP and engaging in orgies in cramped apartments, they always had their sights set on success. Maybe Dan and Ryan were "professional artists,' but he was *an artist*.

Dash lit a cigarette and decided to listen to his voice messages.

"Can you please call us back," said Jade on the line. "Secret misses you. We're all very worried. Call back soon, please!"

Guilt and regret overcame him. The heroin could no longer dilute his inner turmoil. He knew that if he wanted to raise this daughter he'd have to radically change his life. But in this city, with ghosts haunting every corner, he'd never escape. Dash liked to joke about faking his own death as a final work of art; a morbid comment on artworld fame. What fun he would have living off the grid on some tropical island, logging into WiFi at an internet café and reading all the articles and obituaries where people would debate the creative worth of his work and his self-destructive ways. What masochistic joy it would bring to know how people really thought of him! Now he was fairly certain the real thing was coming first.

He put Black Flag's *Damaged* on the boombox. Dash blasted another line of coke up his nose, extra fat, and allowed the menace of Greg Ginn's opening chord progression on "Rise Above" to wash over him. He stood up, started swaying his shoulder side to side, and started thrashing about the room as Rollins' opening lines were shouted into the space. He did a spin move by mentally copying Michael Jackson, before thrashing about side to side as the song reached its one-minute marker.

Jealous cowards try to control! Rise above we're gonna rise above!

Truer words never spoken, Dash thought. The force of Rollins' delivery gave him resolve. "Fuck all of them!" he thought, cooking up two more bags of smack and injecting them into his favorite vein (now entirely bruised and sporadically covered in track marks). He picked up a shoebox that was stuffed full of polaroid photographs. Countless images of people wasted and fucking and shooting cocaine. "The good life," Dash muttered. He tried to understand the art that people saw in these images. He supposed

40

there was a voyeuristic allure to them. "But so do the tabloids," he thought, chuckling, a Red dangling from the corner of his mouth. Dash was in love with language, street language, specifically. It was Burroughs that made him want to be a New York junkie artist. He loved the little secret meanings that Burroughs used to convey their hidden world to one another: "gash," "on the nod," "croakers," Dash recalled fondly. The streets need a language, and the artist turns this language into an art, and the art becomes an icon to the language of the streets. This, he thought, was something to aspire to. Dash wanted to capture a subcultural, criminal zeitgeist in his works. He viewed this as his natural trajectory. He wanted to give this spirit a visual embodiment. He wanted to elevate graffiti, and degrade contemporary art. He wondered if anyone saw that.

He rejected his upbringing. He still hated his mother and had only recently started warming up to his father. Perhaps it was because he recognized his father's propensity for drug use and inability to stay still in himself. He at least understood his father's flaws, his mother was just a domineering, spoiled cunt. He knew his relationship with his family was good gossip fodder, but Dash had never really struggled; not for a moment - not even when he was on the streets. His grandma never let him become the delinquent that he thought of himself as. He was ghetto rich even when he was poor. He'd collect $2000 from grandma and spend 60 percent of it on heroin and 40 percent on cocaine, until he was broke again. He never escaped the accusations of his haters: a rich kid. Dash took another bump of coke off his hand. He never understood why his friends from the IRAK crew didn't mind who he was or where he came from. Most of them were from broken homes and foster care. In a graffiti crew, your identity melts away into your tag. He wasn't Dash Snow, he was SACE. Kunle wasn't Kunle Martins, he was Earsnot.

All that mattered was that you boosted the crew. It was beautiful. Dash should have killed himself back then, he thought to himself. As he sat there, thumbing through the photos and compulsively smoking, he thought of all the ridiculous ways that his work had been sold over the years. NY Magazine called him one of "Warhol's Children," even though he hated Warhol. People used the word "Basquiat" a lot when writing about him. Dash knew that the only thing Basquiat-esque about him was his youth, his propensity for drug abuse, and his aura of imminent death. Basquiat could paint his ass off. Dash could barely draw a circle. Dumping a bump of coke out onto the back of his palm and taking a sniff, coughing outwards with the drip, Dash wished people would see the street language in his work. If there were artists he aspired towards, it was Burroughs and Gysin. The artists that sublimated urban degeneracy, made it a part of the history of art. "Whatever that means," he thought. Having already gone through nine bags of heroin and two and a half grams of cocaine, Dash grew more self-important. Drugs made him delusional. Maybe that's why he loved them.

When Dash started taking these polaroids, he approached them without a plan or preconceptions. It was something he just did. He got wasted and took photographs and did graffiti and crimes. Dash put the photographs aside to prepare a speed ball. He was running lower on drugs than he was comfortable with. It was only 4:30 pm. Dash's heart rate spiked for a moment, a bit of a shock setting in as he realized the near-lethal amounts of drugs he was shooting. It was the worst habit he'd ever had, and it was getting worse. Dash knew drug addicts who had gone homeless. This had never been a worry for Dash. "IRAK,' he muttered, now close to a stupor.

42

Dash mulled over whether to have his dealer make a drop-off. He decided that it'd be better for him to just go outside. He knew it could be the last time to breathe the air of the streets. Dash walked back over to the pile of clothes. He removed the Samhain t-shirt. Looking again at his reflection, he put his right arm to his left rib cage. The strength he had accrued from running around Manhattan and climbing up buildings had withered. He couldn't see his face, covered in beard and hair, and his body was only skin to conceal his bones. It was losing its shape, and its vitality. Dash's tattoos were already starting to feel like a mistake, just another thing that made him a corny *Purple Magazine* art fag. The candy skulls that crossed his chest. "Cocaine" imprinted into his right shoulder with gothic print. Right arm covered in a Raymond Pettibon design; the visage of a cop, a symbol of the authority that Dash despised. Dash realized that he had been crafting a persona ever since he split from home as a teenager. But as the artworld cast him further into that role, he leaned into it more - like a thirsty fool. He did more drugs. He got more tattoos and made himself look even more like a caricature of corporatized bohemia. Dash, staring directly into his pale blue eyes, hacked and coughed. Self-disgust had been a troublesome habit for some time – over time it becomes yet another addiction.

Dash, ever style-conscious, adorned himself in his black cowboy hat, his thrashed black motorcycle boots and a white t-shirt. He blasted three more massive lines of cocaine, finishing off what was left of the 8-ball. Finding his leather gun holster vest on the floor to the side of the bed, he slipped it on. Sending a text message to his dealer, he informed him he'd be over soon to buy seven grams of cocaine and thirty bags of heroin ($290 for the coke, $300 for the junk, always buy in bulk). Dash walked swiftly towards the door and opened it halfway. With one foot in the hallway, he looked back towards the room and noticed ripped pieces of paper littering the floor (the result of half-started collages and Dash's maniacal, drug-induced collecting practice). A profoundly melancholic nostalgia made him lose any desire to leave the room. He called the dealer back while preparing another injection of heroin.

"Yeah...I'm tied up right now. Listen if you come here now, I'll give you an additional $200."

"I'll be there in 10 minutes."

Dash liked looking out for his friends (he didn't know his dealer's name but felt close to him).

Picking up the shards of paper that derailed his outing, Dash was lost in the memories of 2007. It was only two years ago, and yet it felt like it was worlds away. Sitting back on the floor and nodding out, the coke had worn off and the dope was dragging him downwards, into the floor and away from the universe. Near incapacitated, Dash managed to drag himself over to the boombox to put on the Bad Brains' ROIR cassette. As soon as he managed to trigger the play button, he collapsed backwards, on the torn pieces of books and magazines. Into the void...2007 was the year that Dash got comfortable with telling people that he was an artist. It was the last time he felt a sense of openness – of limitlessness, really – about the future. He was already a daily user of heroin, but the drug abuse still felt connected to an ethos of aesthetic experimentation and rejection of the social order. Dash had ideated suicide most of his adolescent and adult life. But, in 2007 he no longer felt the inclination. The drugs made him feel alive. "The Hamster's Nest," Dash thought to himself. "The fucking Hamster's Nest."

Dash should have never let "The Hamster's Nest" become *The Hamster's Nest*. He shivered with this insight. Painfully, Dash remembered a line from that dreadful *NY Magazine* profile (although he'd basically memorized the whole thing, he only ever remembered the part he despised).

Where Goldin and Larry Clark were saying something painful and anxiety-producing about Kids and what happens when they take drugs and have sex in an ungoverned urban underworld, McGinley started out announcing that 'The Kids Are Alright,' fantastic, really, and suggested that a gleeful, unfettered subculture was just around the corner—still—if only you knew where to look.

Dash, nodding along half-heartedly to "Banned in D.C.," realized that this might have been the problem. Ryan's natural propensity for joyous exuberance blunted any self-critical potential and turned them into an appealing image ripe for recuperation. Without that shred of doubt cast upon their debauched activities, they were fashion. "The Hamster's Nest" was born of drug and alcohol-soaked libidinal energy. He and Colen would get set up in a hotel room and felt this primal need to signal how little amenities meant to them. They'd inject heroin, snort coke, eat mushrooms, swallow MDMA, and rip all the pages out of the phone book, covering the room in its discarded paper detritus. Dash and Dan would thrash around the room until everything, sheets, curtains, drapes, and their clothes, were all littered around the floor. But Dash never felt like a hamster doing the "Hamster's Nest," he was just on drugs and being destructive. It was pure.

When he allowed that purity to be recreated at Jeffrey Deitch gallery, he signed the contract of his own co-optation by the asinine New York fashion and art media nexus. Dash opened his eyes and sighed deeply, anger puncturing the walls of opiated bliss. He thought of all the rich New York media faggots drooling over him like he was some kind of delinquent American Hustler, everyone using his image for their own sick pursuits of greed and excess. They told him he should just enjoy the ride. The Bad Brains cassette had ended and all that could be heard was the static of the rolling tape. Dash lit a cigarette. The phone rang.

"Hello Mr. Snow, you have a guest, he won't give his name, can we send him up?"

Dash could barely utter words at this stage, but somehow they got the message. His dealer was walking up the stairs. There was a knock at the door.

"Come on in," Dash muttered, opening the door. In waltzed his dealer, a tall and slightly shouldered brown man of ambiguous ethnicity. He never stayed long.

"What do you need?"

Dash forked over a grand. The dealer handed over two large packages of powder – one light brown and the other off-white. Sitting next to each other on the couch, Dash could barely muster the strength to keep his eyes open; he appreciated his dealer's lack of scruples (he must have known that Dash was already on an overdose quantity of drugs, but still sold him more without question) but didn't like his tendency towards lingering.

"Would you like to do a line?"

Dash did want to do a line, but alone. Nevertheless, he allowed the dealer to take his personal stash out of the front pocket of his Adidas track pants and pour two lines along the table. After snorting one with Dash's $100 bills, he handed it to Dash. "Go ahead my friend," he said through his accent, equally hard to identify as his ethnicity. Dash snorted, but was now jonesing once more for heroin and had to speed this process up. The dopamine rush of the shockingly pure cocaine overwhelmed Dash with an uncontrollable urge to chat. He'd been alone for days, after all.

"How's your beautiful daughter" asked the dealer.

Dash paused, lit a cigarette, nodded and then spoke, "She's amazing. But I'm no kind of father. It's impossible for me to be a dad while living here. Look at me, man. My heart could stop at any fucking moment. Maybe I'd be better off it did."

The dealer's face contorted. He was perturbed. "I see," he said, snorting back to get another drip. "What do you plan to do with this?"

Dash figured that since he didn't even know this guy's name he could speak freely, without worrying about where the information traveled.

"I'm going to do drugs until I die," said Dash. "I'd kill myself, but I don't think I have the stomach for it. You know what I'm saying?"

The dealer, thinking intently, nodded.

"Or… I'm just going to disappear. I have a plan. Whatever comes first."

The dealer looked very uncomfortable and what Dash said clearly freaked him out. He said he was running late. When he was gone, Dash put on Suicide. He always listened to "Ghost Rider" auto-biographically. He worshipped Alan Vega and saw them as being connected somehow. Criminals living lives between comfort and degeneracy, art insiderdom and delinquent outsiderdom. But that was neither here nor there.

Dash prepared a shot of three bags of heroin. He decided it was time to call Jade. It was only about 6 pm. Heroin made his days seem both shorter and longer. No, it was one continuous day. Bouts of sleep were just pauses that felt like one elongated, half-conscious fantasy. Opiated life was a lucid dream. Nothing seemed real, but he was cognizant of the unreality. Dash looked at his right arm. He was in mourning for the pleasures of the body that he experienced with heroin. But all things must come to an end. He went to the refrigerator and took out two beers, a bottle of Amstel Light and a can of Heineken. He laid back on the bed and grabbed the phone off of the receiver. He breathed heavy, and arranged the words that he'd say to the mother of his child. His nerves were shattered but the dope had him steady. He took the last swig from a mostly empty bottle of *Bacardi* rum. Tears formed at the corners of his eyes. He hadn't cried in a long time, and he took this as a good sign. He was still alive. He laid out another line on the nightstand and snorted it back. With his heart palpitating, he dialed Jade's cellphone (it took him a couple tries to remember the right digits). It rang twice. She picked up; Dash could hear people in the background. He thought he heard Hanna's voice, asking if it was indeed him. There was concern in her voice.

"Dash?" said Jade on the other line. "Is that you? Where are you? Are you at the hotel? Are you ok? We're all very worried about you."

Dash paused. He breathed in deep. "Hang on," he said. He walked to the boombox and turned the volume down. Back at the phone now, Dash tried to gather his thoughts. He was shivering and sweating, itching at his nose nervously. "Goodbye. I love you. I'll see you in another world." Dash could hear Secret crying in the background. It hurt him, but he knew she'd be better off. They all would. He hated his parents, and now his daughter would never get a chance to hate him. Maybe that's better. Before Jade could gather her thoughts and reply, he hung up. There were two more rings of the phone, which he ignored.

Dash put his sheets and pillow on the floor, pushing the assorted book and tapes to the side. He put the tape that Leo had made for him on. It opened with the Teenage Jesus and the Jerks song "Orphans." Lydia's howl chilled his almost lifeless body.

Little orphans running through the bloody snow!
Little orphans running through the bloody snow!

Dash prepared a heaving shot of heroin. He needed energy no more. Five bags. His plan was to inject it and see what happens. He was rolling the dice on life and letting fate decide where he goes from here. As the butane lighter dissolved the smack into the water - the smell of burnt hair clogging his nose – he thought about the past. He contemplated the future. Through its blackness, he saw the faintest bit of light. Perhaps the world was opening to him once more. He tied the snake belt around his bicep and slapped the center of his right arm. He found a vein. As he pushed the needle in, he saw Secret behind his eyelids. And Ryan. And Dan. And Jade. And Agathe. And Earsnot. He imagined that they were all crowded around him, embracing him. With the blood mixed in with the dope, he pushed it back in. His adoring ghosts whispered into his ears. They loved him. He fell backwards, and his head slammed on the pillow. He felt nothing as his eyes drooped into the back of his head.

He was sinking. He noticed his heartbeat was slowing, opening up a void inside his body. He sank deeper, the room rose above him. His blood was frozen now. His memories were warm and he was cold...Everything was getting dark, so he closed his eyes. His breathing was belabored. He thought of what death would be like. Perhaps he'd wake up and start a new life in secret. Perhaps his coffin would be empty, and this would all be an elaborate stunt. He'd let those closest to him in on it...Deeper, and deeper, into the void of his barren uninteresting mind. It was beautiful here. Dash knew they would all understand. He was 1000 feet beneath the floor from which he lay. He tried breathing one more time but couldn't quite catch the breath. He stopped trying.

CHAPTER 3

◆ dedo ◆

When he awoke, Dedo's head was so full of physical pain that it felt two sizes too small for his brain. He couldn't breathe. He coughed violently for several minutes until a small amount of blood appeared in his handkerchief. There was no way he could simply fall back asleep. The dreaminess was gone and his brain was turned on. Sickness and alertness were two sides of the same coin. Illness tethered Dedo to waking reality and there was only so much he could do to sever the tie. Not for lack of trying, though.

He got himself out of bed and stretched out. He hacked corrosively, but the phlegm would not be expelled from his throat, denying him much longed relief. Dedo's phlegm was his spiritual nag. A perpetual reminder of the decay of youth. With every strained breath, the mucus at the back of his throat reminded him how meaningless it all was. His art. His success, or lack of it. His own life. It was all so temporary.

All this portended a truly awful day. "I am strong, I am magnetic, I am worthy of your admiration," he thought to himself, stewing in a vacuum of self-deception. Dedo held the mantras of Nietzsche close to his heart. He rotated these mantras in his head and tried to keep them at the forefront of his mind. They gave him the illusion of strength. That was all he had

....and nothing besides!...you yourselves are also this—and nothing besides

He had spent his last bit of money at the bistro the previous night, so a hefty breakfast was now out of the question. Luckily, he had plenty of opium, alcohol, and half a baguette that would keep his body partially nourished throughout the day. He had a commission scheduled for that afternoon, and Pablo was to bring over a poet named Cocteau. Dedo was unfamiliar with the writer, but work is work.

Dedo hoped that this Cocteau would allow him to drink and smoke while he sketched the portrait. He simply could not tolerate a prudish presence. He walked over to the blinds to slide them open and let the sun into his studio. With the window cracked open and the temperate Parisian air drifting in, Dedo hoped for an uplift that would not come. For a man who had experienced so much, he often wondered if he had ever really known one moment's happiness.

Coughing more and more, Dedo gazed out on Montparnasse — the sun's gleam was illuminating the people below as they sipped wine and coffee outside cafés and marveled at his own capacity for survival. It was only a couple of years before drug use almost hanged him permanently. But he was here. He was alive, and though he was belabored, he was breathing in the fresh air of the city below. Was his strength cosmic? Or was it a byproduct of the heroin, morphine, laudanum, and the constant whiskey and brandy he used to dull his pain? An opiated overdrive, perhaps. He took a swig from his tincture of laudanum and closed his eyes while its effects spread out over his body. Within moments the chills had been vanquished, the sweat evaporated, and the aches and pains in his neck and joints were eased. With life returned to him, he stretched down to his feet and held his hands around his workmen's boots, inhaling and exhaling deeply. With each breath, he felt a modicum of strength restored. Synthetic or organic, it mattered not. Dedo had to work and this was the only way.

Dedo had long lived with an awareness that his life would be cut short. And there were times that this knowledge — knowledge that he would only share with Oscar and his closest of confidantes — was spiritually liberating in a way that can *only* be understood by those who have been marked for death. He was morally unburdened by the concerns of ordinary men. He flipped through *Les Chants de Maldoror*, which he kept on his drawing desk by the window. In Lautréamont, Dedo had found a brother with whom he could share his nightmares. He found a master who showed him how to face his ever-approaching death. Dedo opened the book to one of his favorite passages, when Maldoror meets "the Creator" ("Who is the creator?" Dedo constantly asked himself — was it God? Dedo chose to interpret him as the appearance of an all-natural order; that is what Maldoror opposes and sought to destroy).

I am the Most High and yet on one count I remain inferior to men, whom I created with a modicum of sand! Tell them a brazen lie, tell them I never left heaven, have been constantly caught up with the cares of the throne, among the marbles, statues, and mosaics of my palaces

Maldoror defies! He acknowledges the creator but refuses to obey the sanctimony of his divine right! Dedo's pulse elevated as he pondered the dynamic, dropping two more drops of laudanum on his tongue before tilting his head back and grinning. He knew there was no creator. The only thing he had to evade was death; though his excesses were making the hurdles he had to clear higher and higher. He made every painting like it could be his last — and thus, he made every painting like it was a final spell that could alter the world. If art didn't open the path towards salvation and truth, then it wasn't worth it.

When the cough had been replaced by a pleasant itch on the nose, he knew it was time to prepare for the day ahead. He felt a subtle glow of health return to his cheeks as he poured some water onto his hands and splashed it onto his face. Dedo looked at the paintings around him, some finished and others unfinished. Every image was the reflection of a memory. Another painting, another encounter, another version of him. He was still poor, but money couldn't validate what he already knew. Looking from painting to painting, Dedo filled a glass .25 tincture of opium and a shot of whiskey. He put some water in a kettle and waited for it to bubble. He mixed the drugs into the boiling water and stirred a packet of green tea into the mixture. He capped it off with some cream from the fridge, and a teaspoon of sugar.

He looked at the wall across his bed displaying a sketch for his portrait of the Algerian Almaiisa. Letting the opium wash over him, feeling the itch and warmth melting into the pores of his skin, he recalled the way she smelled. Lavender perfume. She wanted to have sex with him but he had doped himself impotent, and coughed blood while trying to masturbate his way to an erection. And she left. The painting implies the narrative, he thought. All that desire and unresolved tension. Dedo was so numbed by his daily drug abuse and excessive drinking that his paintings came to be the only thing that reminded him of his own subjectivity. Free of morality but still full of turmoil and regret, Dedo could no longer count the lies he told himself. He could no longer keep track of the delusions he clung to.

He could read Lautréamont all day, but Maldoror's absence of superego eluded him. Maldoror is free of regret and guilt. Even in his most inebriated states, Dedo couldn't divorce himself from the haunted lingering of regret. Because he wasn't Maldoror. He was a man, a very sick man. The anguish Dedo experienced when his ego demystified itself was immense. He poured more laudanum into the glass and drank it back, gagging on its flavor which initiated another heaving attack of coughing. Blood on his hands. A tear formed at the corner of his right eyelid, which he swiftly brushed aside. He breathed deeply and sat at the chair at his workstation in front of the window and collected himself. Did the artist need to feel a sense of his own death, he asked himself. Is death that one thing that we must know to access that which lies beyond?

Dedo got dressed. He put on his favorite chambray collared shirt, with its blue and white check loose at the sleeves and adorned it with his favorite kerchief, tied loosely around his neck. His faded velvet suit smelled like whiskey, tobacco and opium. There was a cum stain near his left thigh from a blowjob he had received from a prostitute some weeks before. Dedo's eyes zoned in on his portrait of Maude Abrantes, remembering how he had simply painted it over a discarded nude. Having grown bored of the bitter flavor of laudanum, he grabbed his pipe from beneath the desk where he kept it perched against the left side of the chair space. He placed a piece of opium in the bowl. He tried to clear his throat to prevent a coughing fit, and lit a match to the bowl, allowing the pleasant smell of ammonia to suffuse him in anticipation. After exhaling, Dedo coughed persistently for five minutes. His mouth was caked in the flavor of blood. But when the coughing ended, the opium hit him so hard that he almost fell back asleep, eyes drooping as consciousness ebbed and flowed. Dedo's mind traversed through the fog of his memories.

Some of the most contented moments of his life occurred amidst clouds of opium and hashish. It was his best friend Noël Alexandre and his father Paul who became his first patrons, initiating him into an exciting sphere of intellectual camaraderie, libidinal freedom and drugs. Dedo fondly looked back on those nights at the *fumeries* of Montmartre where he smoked opium and cannabis, getting lost in conversations and waking hours later. It was during these times when Dedo first experienced the deprivations of real poverty, having since then lived off the meagre allowance provided by his parents well until his twenties. But Paul introduced Dedo to everyone and soon enough he received almost daily commissions from those who would visit him in his studio at the Bateau-Lavoir. Thanks to these, he found himself able to hustle enough to live. It was a beautiful time. Paul wanted him, Brancusi, and all the others to be mystics, free of the restrictions of class society. "Bourgeois scum," Dedo muttered to himself. He lit the pipe again and inhaled a smaller hit of the opium.

Dedo was in remission from his illness at that point. He was up to his eyeballs in debt, but somehow life went by smoothly. He couldn't sell a painting but still managed to survive. His strife was noble. The copious hash and opium he smoked allowed him to look at objects as portals; if he was able to dilute his analytical mind through chemical alteration, art objects became cracks in reality that he could peek his eyes through and glimpse infinity. As he took another toke from the bowl, Dedo pondered African art — its elegance in form, its beauty untethered to academicism or hackery — and asked himself if his art had ever attained the purity of those objects he'd often buy at flea markets for little more than a few francs, works of the human soul laid bare.

Opium and hashish purified and simplified Dedo's awareness; they melted layers away until all that remained was raw tender emotion and beauty. These sculptures similarly sought irreducible organic form, the artistic gesture minimized as a singular expression. The sculptural masks of the Cameroonian and the Congolese were intercessors that had the cosmic power to protect the individual from the threat of evil spirits that those masks in fact inhabited. Dedo was taken with this concept. In his paintings and sculptures, he sought to turn the human face into the mask of a demonic entity that would nevertheless protect the sitter from that demon. Dedo was now very high, slumping into his chair and basking in an opiated bliss. Something had changed in his work in recent years, he realized. It had become darker. He wondered if perhaps his paintings weren't protecting his sitters from demonic spirits but cursing them with those very devils.

When did it all change, and how? A despair was growing inside of him that was getting increasingly difficult to conceal behind his performance of charm. The memory of one opium night at Pablo's studio persisted. It was 1908. Everyone seemed to be there: Paul, Noël, Juan Gris, Pablo Gargallo, André Salmon, Apollinaire, Max Jacob, Pablo's then girlfriend Fernande Olivier, and an assortment of other beautiful women. Pablo, whose pretentiousness and affectations had always amused Dedo, considered himself to be above the vulgar pharmaceutical grade heroin and morphine that was infinitely more powerful but less seductive. Instead, he was attracted to the opium den setup for its orientalist charm. They had a splendid evening sitting on straw mats around an oil lamp which projected shadows and new forms on the paintings adorning the studio walls. But that night something went horribly wrong. A young painter named Karl-Heinz Wiegels started ranting incoherently. He was raving mad and screamed at everyone in the room with his fists clenched tight, repeatedly pounding them into his chest.

"You homosexual bourgeois scum! I feel you stealing my essence! You seek to sodomize me, you dirty self-important buggers! Pablo! Have you no decency, why — have you brought me into this den of wretched evil!"

The young Wiegels had suffered a mental breakdown after ingesting a heavy cocktail of opium, hash and ether. He simply wasn't built for it, it seemed. Picasso discovered Wiegels hanging from the roof of his studio later that same night. Dedo believed that Pablo never truly forgave himself; he was far more sentimental than most people thought him to be. From there, it seemed their group started to disband. Pablo swore off the use of drugs altogether. Dedo, on the other hand, retreating deeper, came to believe that it was only through opium and alcohol that he could access his genius.

"Dedo!" came from a voice outside. "It's Pablo, I have the young poet here."

Dedo lightly slapped both cheeks in rhythmic unison to wake himself up, wiping the sleep from his eyes and the drool from his cheek. Collecting himself, he walked to the door and let the visitors in. Pablo wore a grey crew neck sweater with wide legged trousers tucked into his work boots.

"You look well!" Dedo could detect the lying in his wavering voice, knowing full well that he looked like a man near death, that is to say, like shit.

"I'd like you to meet Jean Cocteau, a poet. He's looking forward to sitting for you." Dedo extended his hand to the young man, who reciprocated while looking him directly in the eyes with a piercing glance.

"I have admired your paintings for a long time now." Cocteau remarked. Dedo mouthed an inaudible reply. Picasso made to leave.

Although he wasn't familiar with this Cocteau, he had heard enough to think it wise to treat him well. He was impressed by the poet's sartorial presentation. He looked deadly handsome, immaculately dressed in a navy-blue suit, neatly pressed over a white collared shirt. A seemingly unused white silk pocket square was tucked into the front pocket. Cocteau's facial structure was rigid and full of color and vitality; his cheek bones were razor sharp. The poet's hair stood up on his head in a glorious tuft, looking so dense that you'd wonder whether you could even move your fingers through it. Through the haze of opium and laudanum, the effects of which were now yielding a light nausea in the pit of his stomach, Dedo found himself equally enchanted and resentful of the young poet. This young man had the whole world ahead of him, it was all his for the taking.

"A drink?"

"A little whiskey sounds splendid," Cocteau replied cheerfully.

Dedo nodded. "How about some opium. Smoke some with me before we start?

Cocteau, still standing, looked up sharply. There was intrigue in his eyes. "No, just the whiskey for now, thank you. But please, don't hold yourself back on my account. I want you to draw under the conditions that you're most comfortable with."

"This self-important little queer," Dedo thought to himself.

"Very well, I will smoke and then assemble my easel. Give me a few moments."

Cocteau strolled around the studio while Dedo prepared his pipe, stopping in front of each painting, casting his eye over specific details. It was clear to Dedo that Cocteau was no fake. He understood and appreciated art. Dedo diverted his attention from the poet and put another piece of opium back in the bowl. He took a heaving hit into his lungs and held onto it before exhaling.

"Ahemm, ahemm, ackkkkk!" Dedo was so short of breath it felt as if he was being strangled by a man twice his strength. Humiliated, he tried to prevent further coughing. But it was too late. Cocteau rushed over to his side and put a hand on his back and squeezed his hand.

"Are you alright?" Cocteau asked.

Croaking and barely able to utter a syllable, Dedo managed to plead for water.

Cocteau filled a glass from the sink and handed it to him. After a few sips, Dedo managed to collect himself. The problem with opium is that there was a momentary lapse between inhalation and high. But he was numb and warm enough now.

"Perhaps you'd like me to return some other time?"

"Nonsense," he said. "Go sit in that chair in the light and I'll set up."

Dedo looked intently at this gorgeous fop of a poet. As he started sketching the contours of his face, he cropped out the entire background to have his image occupy most of the canvas grid. Dedo could feel himself wanting to emphasize this man's beauty, but also to express the envy for that beauty. It became clear that the resentfulness he felt rooted in a realization that despite being only five years apart in age: Dedo felt ancient in his presence.

"What do you write about?" He asked.

"It's hard to describe. I want to emphasize beauty, you see...I don't like to edit my work. Even if it's incorrect, I prefer it be the original. Because that's what I felt when I wrote it."

Dedo pondered this idea; he reckoned it was a good one. He took a swig of laudanum to cap off the opium, and Cocteau furrowed his brow.

"Don't squint" Dedo snapped.

"My apologies"

Cocteau's form was starting to metastasize in the sketch–or at least, Dedo's vision of Cocteau.

"And you have a connection with Proust?" Dedo asked.

"He's taken an interest in me," Cocteau replied. "But I write from my blood and lust. I am no intellectual."

"Maybe this kid really has something..." Dedo thought.

"What do you like to read?" Cocteau asked.

"Lautréamont is my constant companion." The sketch was nearing completion, but he realized his rendering of Cocteau's nose was rather timid.

"Do you have a taste for the wicked?" The young poet asked.

"I don't see evil in Maldoror," he said. "He's free. He understands that to live a mortal life is to be utterly liberated. This is the source of his power."

"But you are so young. You mustn't think so bleakly! Surely you must see what is happening all around us – *we* are the future."

Anxiety swirled upwards to Dedo's chest. He wanted Cocteau out of this studio as swiftly as possible. Dedo paused from drawing, taking another hit off the pipe. He coughed profusely for another three minutes. But this time, he looked directly into Cocteau's eyes, and as he did so, communicated something that he dared not say. He finished the drawing.

"We're all done here for now."

"Splendid," said Cocteau, getting up.

"I shall see you soon, I hope? Please do take care of that cough, the opium can't be helping."

Dedo now had a complex array of emotions about this poet: admiration, contempt, and brutal, ugly envy. He wanted what Cocteau had, he wanted his life and his future.

"I assure you Cocteau, there will come a time in your life where things won't seem so perfect. And I hope that you too have something to mitigate this tragedy." He replied in parting.

Cocteau nodded, shook Dedo's hand, and left.

Dedo poured himself an entire glass full of whiskey and gulped it down as he prepared the painting. As he painted Cocteau's face, eyes looking out towards the left of the canvas and away from the viewer's eye, he was overwhelmed by the sense of his finitude. For years he had been able to keep his illness at bay and suppress his physical pain. But this fiercely confident young poet perturbed him. He could smell the rot, the stench of death.

In this painting, he tried to deny Cocteau his beauty. He wanted to steal it for himself, but he couldn't. He couldn't grasp the poet's youth nor his future. He knew it wasn't his. This was the power of the work, he realized - its allure and melancholy. He was withering away. He would deteriorate. He didn't have much time left. He finished the painting and took another throat full of opium.

Murderous rage began to simmer. Cocteau had inspired something deeply dark in him.

He came to when there was a knock at the door. Cocteau had returned for his painting.

"I'm excited to see what you came up with."

Dedo pointed to the easel, taking delight in the disappointment that was instantly smeared across Cocteau's face. Clearly he was displeased.

"It's splendid, just splendid....I didn't realize you'd make it so large, it may be rather outsized for my purposes. But the ambition of it is fantastic."

While Dedo appreciated Cocteau's well-heeled manners and grace, he couldn't shake the feeling that he was being lied to.

"Why don't you keep it, Monsieur. Keep it for your shows. It's beautiful, you should keep it."

If Dedo couldn't have his future, then Cocteau couldn't have his painting. They shook hands and parted ways. He collapsed onto his bed, while his breathing became interspersed with more painful coughing. He had a slight urge to stalk Cocteau into the night, follow him into an alley, and cut his throat, leaving the poet bleeding out behind a dumpster somewhere. But this was a passing thought, and he was physically incapable of such ferocity anyway. He was aware of his body's frailty. He noticed the world getting darker and his losing grasp of it. But he wasn't ready to go just yet. If there was more to see, then he would see it.

CHAPTER 4

✦ Zoë ✦

Heroin saved Zoë's life. Her existence had been fragmented into two parts; life before heroin and life during heroin. The second half of the story, while not without its downsides, was the one in which she felt whole. She hadn't lost her looks, her talent, or her mystique. On the contrary, heroin only accentuated the unique beauty she was blessed with. It gave her a dreaminess, a veil of seductive allure.

Zoë had been aware of her beauty since she was young. And every time she caught her reflection in the mirror, she became more aware of it. Her cheeks were pointed and sharp, while at the same time delicate and feminine. Her eyes were so far apart that men could fit their pointed fingers spread out between them. Her lips, plump and pink, were built to smoke and to suck. She often wondered, had she never used heroin, would she have ever been anything more than a beautiful woman artists wanted to fuck, wear on their arms and then cast aside, old and withered. But on junk she glowed, she found her voice, and, more importantly, her confidence to claim that voice. Heroin made Zoë an artist.

Zoë had found her moment. Nearing the end of her young adulthood, she felt new power flowing through her. By the time she turned 30, she knew that her genius would be recognized. This was it. With heroin as her faithful companion, she would claim the respect that she deserved. She would be treated with the seriousness befitting a mind as singular as hers. She had been on the cusp of the real thing for so long. She recalled all those concerts, where people applauded her beautiful piano performances. But that music was not hers, it did not come from her.

Until now, Zoë was merely a vessel through which someone else's genius manifested; the muse, the model and the actress. That's not what an artist is, she thought: that's a prop. She would be a prop no more. She would make the world understand the beauty that lived inside her; she would unleash it upon them and they would have no choice but to know that beauty was her own. The world would know. *They have no choice.*

She had spent the entire previous decade in the shadow of a man she adored. Edouard taught her everything she knew but did not respect her. He taught her about art. He brought her into the creative process of his filmmaking. They wrote a novel together (albeit, not a particularly remarkable one). He imbued her with political consciousness. He showed her how to fuck. But what was she to him? She knew exactly what. A trophy. A piece of eye candy that he could use to dust off the decay of his own ailing body, to impress his sycophant friends.

While inside her, Edouard could grasp that which already had drifted away from him. With him inside her, she felt important. Oh, how she craved importance. A successful man always had a certain shine to him, she thought. Yet Edouard was denied the kind of fame that he craved. He was *old*. When they met, he was already in his 70s. He was still charming, and the most brilliant man she had met. But his political rigidity made him brittle and hurt him artistically. Jonas Mekas, Edouard's closest of friends, attributed Edouard's orthodox Marxism as the source of their collaborative failure – *Guns of the Trees*. Mekas, that "infallible" bag of bones that looked at Zoë contemptuously and saw in her little more than a sad, pathetic junkie, wasn't entirely wrong about Edouard. Typical of his generation, he was sometimes shockingly unaware of his own bourgeois moralism. But it went deeper than that, Zoë thought. Edouard was all intellect. He lacked a transcendent dimension. He was not, she slowly realized, a *true* artist. Edouard suspected this about himself, and over time this insecurity made him hellish to be with. She satiated his pain for as long as she could. She did what a 20 something model and actress girlfriend was supposed to do. She made him feel powerful. She hung on his every word. She fucked him so good and so long that his eyeballs rolled into the back of his head. She followed his advice.

Eventually, Zoë wondered whether her relationship with him was worth it. Had she given up everything for him? The four years that they were together felt like a lifetime. She had so many reasons to leave him she could not remember one. Soon she met Robert and married him. She took his name. She liked how it sounded. "Zoë Tamerlis Lund." With Robert, it was easier. He was a professional — an engineer and a technician, a craftsman — who didn't need to have his ego stroked. He was secure. She could love him without being subsumed by him. He cared for her. He let her be herself. He accepted her, addiction and all. With him, Zoë felt comfortable to try, and fail. And fail again. With heroin, she never felt alone. And with Robert, she never felt like a junkie.

71

She spent '85 to '90 in the wilderness, hustling for fame and the recognition she was owed. She grew tired of people treating Kathy Acker like a goddess and her like a model with one movie credit. She wished she hadn't taken the part in that Larry Cohen film. Her stint on *Miami Vice* paid for rent and dope. This was when she started using daily.

And it was strange: the more heroin she used, the more she felt like a real person. Her experience with the drug was far from the horror stories people told kids to keep them clean. Granted, she wasn't destitute. She wasn't rich either, but her modeling contracts and Robert's love and support assured her a degree of comfort and mobility.

With all that empty time and pleasant boredom, she pumped her veins full of dope… And dreamed and drifted through the corners of her psyche. She started writing down her dreams. And what she wrote was beautiful, she thought, because her dreams were. So were her vulnerability and her tenderness and her flaws - they were beautiful too. Heroin wasn't cutting her off from emotion. On the contrary, it made all her feelings – pain and pleasure, contentment and sadness, excitement and anger – beautiful. She did not use heroin to numb her pain, but to be able to confront her pain. And in confronting it, she saw its beauty. Everything on dope was perfect.

She remembered a line from a story she'd recently written. She named it "Cul de Sac," like the Van Morisson song (but she wasn't sure if the reference was conscious or not).

Nodding. On the most illegal of drugs. She balanced her head against the building and let her eyes close over the sky.

72

On junk, life itself became the raw material of her art. Junk taught her how to live life as an artist, and how to convert her art into her life.

She wanted to believe that Abel saw her differently than the other men. There was something interesting about Abel, she felt. Abel was so fiercely confident in his artistic vision and masculinity that female genius didn't seem to alarm or intimidate him. Zoë sometimes wished that she stayed with him and continued to work with him after *Ms. 45*. She was proud of that film. She loved how she looked in it and appreciated how Abel saw her through his lens. She remembered walking into the audition. She assumed that his mind was full of lascivious thoughts towards her. But when she spoke and delivered the lines he gave her the part immediately. Whatever fire scorched within her, Abel sensed it. She could have easily become his muse, but she didn't want to get swept up in his creative vision. She feared that she would only be able to define herself in relation to Abel; she couldn't allow that.

Zoë came to and it was already nighttime. She was in a bra and panties, sitting up in her bed. Her syringe had folded itself beneath the sheets. She felt her hands around her flesh to make sure she didn't get pricked anywhere. Two whole hours were gone. She grabbed her pack of Parliament Lights from her nightstand, flicked the lamp on, and lit one of the cigarettes, exhaling smoke rings around the dimly lit room.

"There is no lost time" she said to herself. She was prone to vivid internal dialogues, and heroin crystallized them. My god, heroin. She adored it. Its taste, and the way its taste was different depending on the drug's color. She loved being cloaked in its warmth. Once gripped in its loving embrace, heroin unlocked parts of her mind that she didn't know existed; it synchronized her thoughts and filled her daydreams with so many new representations. She could see *everything*: it made things so clear. My god, she thought, I'll never give it up.

The windows in the apartment she shared with Robert on E. 10th St. were open, and there was a chill in the room. She walked over to the window to open it all the way, and a blast of cold winter air sent a feeling of bliss through her body. The East Village outside was quiet. She stuck her head out the window. Down the block, near 1st Avenue, she saw a lineup of junkies meeting their man. Her comrades. There was nobility to these men and women, these junkies. They were so tethered to the chain of the city, she thought. They were as important to the myths of the city as the cops, bureaucrats and whores. She heard a small commotion outside the bedroom.

The main living space was painted entirely in jet black and looked dark even under full daylight. The walls were covered with film posters. *Taxi Driver. Straw Dogs. Band of Outsiders.* Above the TV hung a massive Richard Prince Marlboro Man print, tactically placed in front of the smoke hatch. Robert cut himself shaving and cursed. He was dressed in a brown, dated disco suit with a white collared shirt underneath, its buttons unfastened and chest hair exposed. He had one of those "ugly-handsome" faces that Zoë coveted. He wore his ugliness well, with masculine pride, which emanated libidinal energy. Their relationship might have looked strange to onlookers, but Zoë loved him deeply.

"Are you ok, sweet?"

"You're not dressed, we're already running late."

"For what?" She knew exactly where they were supposed to be, but her mysterious and forgetful bit made him tender. It worked every time. "Were we supposed to go somewhere tonight?"

Zoë had a strange relationship with lying and manipulation. It was second nature to her, even before she became a heroin addict. It was just so easy to get away with little falsehoods when you looked like her. Deeply insecure before growing into her beauty, Zoë was fascinated with her own talent for distortion. Looking at Robert now, she knew she could say anything and he'd just let it slide. Lying was intoxicating and she seldom felt any guilt about it.

Robert was dabbing a piece of toilet paper to sop up the blood when he looked at her in the mirror. He furrowed his brow, lowering his voice to convey his playful disbelief.

"Oh you forgot, now did you?"

"I did, I totally forgot" Zoë giggled a bit before cupping her hands over her mouth, knowing full well that Robert was fully aware of her tricks. "Where were we to go?"

"Well, my love," Robert said, still doing his faux-stern accent that she adored so much. "We had plans to meet Paul Rachman for dinner… And after dinner, we were going to see Cronenberg's adaptation of *Naked Lunch*."

Zoë had in all honesty been dying to see what Cronenberg had done with one of her favorite books. But perhaps she could use that to her advantage.

"Oh my god!" exclaimed Zoë. "How could I have forgotten? Yes, well I guess I'll throw something on, it's just..."

Robert turned away from the mirror and towards Zoë, looking at her full of love and forgiveness. "What's the matter, sweet? You not feeling well or something? I tried to get your attention for 15 minutes an hour ago, so I assumed you were feeling peachy fucking keen?"

Zoë didn't like when Robert joked about her heroin use. It was sacred to her, but she couldn't get him to understand that. It would only make him more concerned about her addiction. Zoë knew he was worried but kept it to himself to avoid alienating her.

"Well, it's just I want to get this script done, my love," said Zoë.

Robert looked mildly disappointed.

"It might be nice to have the space to myself tonight, Abel is really excited about what I've written and what he's been able to shoot so far. I'm in a groove, I feel something powerful. I don't want to stop. Won't you have a nice time seeing your pal tonight?"

Robert sighed, and kissed her on the forehead, before leading her out of the bathroom. The bleeding in his cheek had stopped.

"You write. I'll go see the film and report it back to you."

"Or maybe you can go meet a wet 20-year-old slut desperate for proximity to the film industry, baby, fuck her for me?" Zoë giggled.

"I really don't like those jokes anymore."

She loved how serious he could be. Like a father, in his eyes she was utter perfection. She sometimes wished she didn't love heroin so much, because he deserved more of her love.

She poured a glass of wine. "Do you want me to order you a pizza?" Robert asked her.

"No honey, but maybe you could leave some cash," she replied. "I might want to go out and get some takeout. Just, maybe, $100, or so? I don't have any cash."

Robert glanced up at her sharply, "You're already out? You just bought 10 bags yesterday! Are you sure this isn't getting out of control?"

She had never heard him question her use like this, and it worried her. "Don't start with me Robert. I'm in the creative process, this is how I create."

He leaned his elbows on the table to feign discontent. She walked up to him, and pulled him back towards her. She unfastened his belt, and grabbed his cock out of his pants, pulling it through the fly.

"Zoë I don't have much time, Paul is already waiting on me." "Shhh," she purred, before inhaling his entire cock to the back of her throat, sucking it in so deep that he was wheezing like an arthritic man trying to walk up the stairs. In two minutes he ejaculated into her mouth. She swallowed.

"Have fun with Paul, baby," kissing him on the lips. He pinched her ass, kissed her back, and was almost out the door before relenting. He turned around, "Before I forget," and slapped $300 on the kitchen table. "Just please be careful, my love," he said. "I don't want you to be around that street scum all the time, so please make it last."

She sat back at the kitchen table for a moment, basking in its open space and listening intently to its silence. And she called her man.

"Yeah?" she heard the thick Brooklyn accent she most associated with pleasure and reward.

"Hello beautiful," said Zoë. "Was wondering if you were holding what I need?"

"How much do you need?"

"Whatever you want to give me for $300." There was momentary static on the phone. Her man was taking a moment to decide how much to fuck her over.

"Three grams good?"

She pondered for a second. It was half a gram less than she was paying him for, but who was she to argue? She lit a cigarette, and decided to barter, a bit.

"That sounds great, but I'm a bit busy here right now. Perhaps you could deliver it to the apartment?"

He sighed a bit, under his breath. "One hour."

"You're a prince."

The line clicked out. Zoë walked to her nightstand and grabbed the last baggie of junk she had saved. She gathered her works and went to the kitchen. She emptied the packet of dope onto the spoon and cooked it with a Bic lighter. She fixated on the aroma as it smoked and crackled. She imagined herself in an occult ritual, between two realities. She wrapped a medical tie around her right arm, rubbing and slapping it until a bright blue vein pulsated outward - ready to be the vessel for her companion. She extracted the cooked junk and gently pricked her vein, watching the blood ooze back into the syringe like an elegant ballet of matter. She pushed it in, pulling the syringe out upon injection. Its warmth creeped on her, and her thoughts sharpened and clarified. *Perfect. Just perfect...*

Zoë walked to the desk in the living room. It was covered in ephemera. Film and fashion magazines. Framed pictures of family, friends and wild nights. She picked one up and looked at it intently - she was inhaling a large line of cocaine as Grace Jones laughed behind her. The picture must have been taken from the Danceteria. Zoë never enjoyed those parties like her friends did. She preferred her private world. There were books: Burroughs, Deleuze's *Cinema 1*, a Tarkovsky film stills book, Syd Field's *The Foundation of Screenwriting*. The typewriter was at the center of all the clutter, half-written and discarded pages crumpled around it. She was doing rewrites for *Bad Lieutenant*, and she felt this was a special piece of work. She was in a near constant state of excitation due to her belief that it was in this screenplay that she would make something important.

It's a story about corruption, faith, and redemption. Zoë's view of the film was very specific, and she wasn't even sure if Abel saw

79

it the same way. For her, it's not the Lieutenant's drug abuse, misogyny or violence that make him "bad." It's his loss of faith, without faith his suffering is futile. He is denied catharsis because he has no higher power to commune with or take refuge in. This is what Zoë wanted to give her character: catharsis. The faith that she had never lost sight of. A connection to the spiritual realm that she herself had always lived with one foot within. When he pulls two young women over and jacks off to their tits, he's begging for God to see him and to punish him. When he smokes heroin with a dealer, played by Zoë herself, he does so to build walls between him and all that is outside. But he's misusing the drug. Heroin should open the floodgates. Heroin can be an access point to God, but only if you are willing to embrace God's existence and love.

This is why, Zoë thought (nodding out a bit, with her fingers on the typewriter), the Bad Lieutenant needs to let the nun's rapists escape, and subsequently accepts his death as a mortal man. This thought alone brought a tear to Zoë's cheek. Abel might have a different notion of this story, but that didn't matter to her. This was meaningful to her. Her buzzer rang.

"Hello?"

"It's me." Zoë grabbed the cash and buzzed him up. The transaction was quick.

Zoë couldn't wait. She immediately went over to her works and fired up three more bags. Clearly, her addiction was worsening. She shuddered to think of what she'd do if she ever ran out of money. But would she trade this feeling to eliminate that fear? Never.

Never. Never. "Why trade the absence of fear for perfection?" she thought to herself. "I am not a coward."

She arose from her nod. She felt like scratching underneath her nose. Her eyes were watery. She got up from the table to dab water on her face. It felt refreshing and restorative. She thought more about the script. She had some thoughts about its final scene. The Bad Lieutenant needs to be gunned down in his vehicle. We will never recognize the gunman. His identity doesn't matter. It's murder as absolution. "Yes," she thought. "That's perfect." Zoë dialed Abel's number to share the idea with him. No answer.

She wanted another shot, but worried that she was overdoing it. Instead, she prepared a piece of tin foil, emptying a packet of dope out onto it. She rolled a dollar bill into her mouth, tin foil in her right hand, the lighter in the left. She lit underneath the foil and sucked the fumes into the dollar bill. She held the fumes in for a full minute and then inhaled. The smell of burnt hair permeated the air. She knew she should get some work done, so she slapped her cheeks awake and walked back to the typewriter.

She returned to that last scene. Without success. She wasn't frustrated, she needed to enjoy her bliss. She needed to let the truth wash over her. Instead, she pulled out a story that she had been working on. It was a story inspired by a painting by a Flemish master that she had seen in a museum as a child. It was a painting about how art and life are two separate worlds, and the roads that must be traveled if one is to traverse the distance. Heroin, of course, was Zoë's path to the sublime. If there was any other way for her she would have taken it. But there wasn't. The sublime was worth dying for.

The words... They came to her, now.

When very young, I saw a painting in a museum. It was Flemish and the painter died a long time ago. In the painting, my sister seems to pray. Her hands touch just like so. A candle burns so close to that absolute bare touch that the fingers glow with the heat-light of its flame. Bled into translucence, my sister's hands are blood-stained-glass over fire. Tending to the flame, hands lose weight to light, gain glow to heat, burn pain in time.

I know her face.

CHAPTER 5
◆ purgatory ◆

An over-populated jazz club. Temporally ambiguous. Loud. Different styles of jazz music on at the same time. A sense of sadness. A sense of chaos. A sense of unease and tension.

...

Here, where time is meaningless, there's *always* music in the air. An entire history of jazz — all its styles, permutations, and generic offshoots — play simultaneously. The good (swing, bebop, modal jazz, free jazz), the bad (jazz fusion, jazz funk, latin jazz) and the ugly (jazzcore, nu-jazz, acid jazz) all play at the same time all the time and most of the cats here go mad trying to block that shit out. They all have their own opinions about what this thing of theirs is supposed to be – and yet they can't escape the incessant noise of what they believe to be perversions of that very thing. You think Cecil Taylor, a recent arrival it seems, wants to hear electric guitar noodlings mucking up the perfection of this thing? God no. It's tense as a motherfucker in here.

There's fights breaking out all the time while they wait for the barman who never seems to show up. Can't even get a decent whiskey up in this joint. It's hot and cold at the same time, never comfortable. And where does the music even come from? You can never even see the fucking stage. There's not enough instruments either, they all quarrel and bicker about who gets to play what but they can't never remember if it's their turn. It's one perverse purgatory, no doubt, but one no less tortuous than any other. It is what it is. You got to pay your dues. These are jazz men, they know all about that. It's their motto. You want to be the band leader then you have to put the time in as a session man. You have to learn to take that abuse. But even so, lots of these cats don't realize how long their suffering might endure. And fewer of them consider the idea that it might actually never end.

They all here though. Miles. Duke. Louis. Monk. Dizzy. Ella. Ayler. Mingus. Ornette. Billie. Dolphy. Pharaoh. And not a single one of them has crossed over. Not one of these damn players has done what needs to be done (whatever that might be) to escape this dank, dark, cramped club that seemingly has less space every time a cat blinks. The vaguest sense of unreality permeates the club. Is it even a club? Who knows. They try not to think about it. But if you stare straight at any one object or thing for too long a time, the room seems like it's moving. It flutters a bit, you see, like it's not a physical structure but a hallucination.

No rest for the wicked, indeed. And this thing, jazz, it is wicked. It's an assault on the senses when done right. It raises ghosts (but not these ghosts). There's a hierarchy on the other side; a clear distinction between the real motherfuckers and the pretenders. In here though, in this club washed in acidic light and cigarette stench and piss - no one could ever find the bathroom - there are no kings. Miles himself was just another face in the crowd. Sun Ra wasn't on his way to Saturn; in fact, he barely ever stands up. He's just sitting there waiting.

And the shit that happens here, it happens over and over. It's like a perpetual state of déjà vu. Miles Davis gets caught getting his dick sucked by some session man he knows from back in the day by Betty, and Betty socks it to him something fierce! Never mind that they already been divorced, there's nothing to do here but be enraged! Betty cracks Miles over the head with a bar stool. Miles smacks Betty around. And they scream! And then it keeps happening. Who can tell how many times? There's no time, remember? It takes every jazz man in the room to prevent Billie and Nina from tearing each other to shreds when the issue of "Strange Fruit" comes up; Nina was sure that her version was the best but Billie was having none of that and they some rowdy broads. Mingus is always telling the players that they're just cogs in a white man's machine, and everyone keeps trying to tell him that there ain't no machine in here! "We just dead, motherfucker!" But Mingus won't listen, he wants to hold onto what he lost. He grasps tight those philosophical bedrocks that made him a man, because if he wasn't still a man he wouldn't know what else he could be. Everyone here grasps tight to what once was, it's too damn scary to just let go.

Chet Baker edges through the crowd again and again. He's sick with the need. He asks everyone but no one is ever holding. And it just happens on loop. He's never ok. He never gets nice. He's always withdrawing: sweating, shaking, aching, pleading. The other thing that happens here is conversations. The same conversations play on repeat, like a skipping vinyl. Ornette and Albert debate the meaning of harmolodics endlessly, and never seem to land on a fixed meaning for the word. Coleman assumes

87

his definition is fixed. Ayler has his own spin on things. They go back and forth, back and forth, until one is screaming at the other. These cats never learn. Dizzy is always ready to lecture about jazz and the "movement for justice," – and Miles is always ready to tell the ol' man: "The only role for jazz is to make me king." Ol' Louis Armstrong defends his singing to anyone who will listen. Most of them scoff at his insistence. He sings over and over and it's like being trapped in an automobile commercial. But there are no spells here. Just these legendary cats who still act like they got something to prove.

Lots of war stories shared, too. Talks about the good old days. Discussions about when jazz mattered and when they were masters of their art. It's tragic really: from a god in life to a fool among the dead. There is no hierarchy here. Death is repetitive and banal. It flattens greatness.

They all love and miss drugs though. They can never find them here. They just talk about them. Cannabis. Cocaine. LSD. And *heroin*. These cats love their junk, they talk about it like it's some kind of magic elixir. They talk about it like heroin is itself the lubricant of jazz. Not everyone agrees, of course. Some of these players think the drug is pure poison. They are glad it's not here with them, wherever they might be. Coltrane, the master himself, thinks that if he had never gotten off the junk, then he would have never become 'Trane. But Bird, he disagrees. Shit, he virulently disagrees. No one can tell for how long these conversations go on (are they even happening at all?). Where the hell are we anyways? Bird and 'Trane are huddled together into a corner. It's hard to see them through the crowd, but they're there. Bird looks well-coiffed in an immaculate three-piece suit, but his eyes are sunken and he's shivering. He's still sick, he carried the sickness here with him from back on the other side. 'Trane's wearing a crisp clean polo shirt with some oversized trousers. He appears spry and engaged, but also unsure. As unsure as anyone else.

'Trane: I pray for you Charlie. I really do.

Bird: Pray for yourself, John. I don't need none of that bullshit. Look at this, you prayed and I didn't. And yet we both stuck in this stankin' ass club in the middle of god knows where. Prayers won't save me…shit, they ain't even saved you. Shove it up your ass. God damn I need a shot, do you know if anyone is holding?

'Trane: You're asking me this again? You asked me this question an infinite number of times, Bird, and you keep asking me. Why?

Bird: Man, fuck you, John! I know I keep asking and I will keep asking cuz I'm hurtin' motherfucker! Besides you always respond the same damn way your own self.

Trane: I suppose that's true, Charlie. I suppose that's true. Have you talked to Dizzy at all? Or is he still avoiding you.

Bird: I haven't talked to him since he got here. Brothers, that's what he used to say we were. Of course, it's convenient to call us brothers when I was the greatest musician on the fucking planet. Dizzy needed my horn blowing. But now, here in this place, that nigga doesn't even wanna talk to me.

'Trane: You're not the most pleasant person to be around when you're in need like this, Charlie.

Bird: Well, find me what I need then, motherfucker…You think I like being sick?

'Trane: I know you don't. I know I didn't. That's why I turned myself over to faith and love, my man.

Bird: Oh here we go again…

'Trane: Even if it has become a footnote to the history of our thing, I feel proud that I freed myself of that affliction.

Bird: You ain't better than me, John. We both here. We just some dead motherfuckers who blew our horns real well. You know how I started, I couldn't keep up, I had fuckin Jo Jones throw a damn cymbal at me. Humiliation became the source of my ambition. And what did I do? I shot dope and I practiced. And practiced and shot more dope. And by the end of that process, by god, Jo Jones couldn't keep up with me. Jazz is struggle, and I needed the obstacles presented by my excesses to carry me through every one of those hard living years.

'Trane: I wouldn't have ever reached my level if I hadn't decided to get that poison out of my system, Charlie. It was holding me back, man. Miles kicked me out his band. I was sick all the god damned time or falling asleep on the damn stage. So I made the decision. I went to my mother's home in Philadelphia, and I told everyone I loved that I'd sweat the poison out. I swore to them, and I prayed to God! I put myself in a goddamned room for two weeks and I didn't leave. My family, they prayed for me, and they brought me water. I faced the sickness, I came face to face with every demon. I stared them in the face and when I saw through

90

them. And I saw God, and God embraced me. He told me that I was put on this Earth to make life more beautiful with music, that my music carried, if not his grace, then some kind of grace.

Bird: And you believed him? That's the sorriest thing I ever heard. God didn't tell you shit. You were just a bottomed out fiend telling himself bedtime stories to get through the hell of it. All due respect, but every motherfucker on the block say the same shit. "By the grace of God!" There ain't no god, man. There's flesh and there's blood and there ain't nothing holy about it. Only two holy motherfuckers on this earth. Jazz and junk.

'Trane: You say these things Charlie but any man with love in his heart can pierce right through your self-deception. It's so clear. You're lost man, and I worry here that you'll never be found.

Bird: To hell with being found, I don't need it. I thrive in the darkness. I was always in the dark, in the mist. And what happened? And you over here acting like you better than me? Hah, hell no man. In a room full of the best to ever do this shit, no one's better than me. Legend and myth are all that matters. Imagine creating the most ferocious sound in the history of music and barely earning enough to keep a roof over your head. When legend is all you have, you best make it a legend worth telling! I earned enough to keep up a dope habit and to eat well, but it was never about being a big career man. Record execs are blood thirsty vampires, they drank from me every chance they got.

'Trane: That's not true. How could anyone think the loss of their own dignity is a rebellion against the man? The man enslaves you because you can't fend for yourself. The man enslaves you because you're already enslaved to his product. No one's denying your greatness, Charlie. No one could. I'm talking about you, as a man – holding yourself back in life and even in death still. You are the faithful servant of a poison that will never love you as much as you love it. You're in love with your own master. An Uncle Tom for a spike and a spoon.

At this insult, Bird stands up, stares 'Trane right in the face, and slaps him across the mouth. Elvin Jones and Max Roach run across the room to intervene. But 'Trane, steely and resolved, waves them off.

'Trane: I'm sorry, Charlie. That was out of line.

Bird: Not so godly now, nigga.

'Trane: I'm just trying to understand.

Bird: What's there to understand, John? You thought you needed to get rid of the junk and find god to evolve the art form, I'm saying I did junk and I perfected it. Everything you did was a fool's errand because all it was, was a kink of something that was already perfect. Bebop was perfect. And I was its perfection.

'Trane: Nothing is perfect, Charlie. Perfection isn't a state of being, it's the quest for something higher. It's in that search for God. For truth. For love. *A Love Supreme*. That's perfection. *A Love Supreme* was the sound of me searching for that perfection, in God. A Universal God, you see? God can be anything, he's in us, whoever we are.

Bird: There ain't nothing in us besides fragility and loose guts, my man. The only perfection I've ever found was in a syringe and in a solo on my sax. I found perfection on "Parker's Mood." And I was high as a kite when I recorded that track, man! Perfection is a frenetic state! It's like religious fervor, except it's real! You can hear it!

'Trane: Your arrogance holds you back! I had to free myself of my vices and ego to become the best artist that I could be. *A Love Supreme* is my gift to humanity, and for it I was rewarded.

Bird: Oh man, I have a lot to say about this. *A Love Supreme* is your gift to crackers drawn to it for its peacenik bullshit. They mean less to me than the shit on my shoe. The only reward a jazz man gets is the music itself. Or a drink and a shot. I can never find any here in this club. Man, I feel awful.

'Trane: And I feel right as rain, isn't that something to aspire to? Feeling ok, free of any chemicals and full of love and God?

Bird: I don't think you've freed yourself of your ego, John. I think you're just another saxophone blowing egomaniac, same as me. Just because you replaced the vice of dope with the vice of god doesn't make you one bit different from me.

'Trane: God isn't a vice.

Bird: So says you, negro. But if you were such a holy rollin' man, why'd you leave your wife? Why'd you leave Naima holding the bag? What kind of holy man runs off on Naima and has two boys with another woman?

At this insult, 'Trane breaks his spiritual posture and furiously stands up and slaps Charlie right across the face. The scene from earlier is repeating itself, flipped in reverse. Again, the other jazz men rush into diffuse. But unlike 'Trane's reserved and contained demeanor, Bird just laughs right in his face, clearly gleeful that he was able to get his heir to show some fire.

Bird: It's good to see there's still some fight left in you boy!

'Trane: Don't call me boy, I'm not some kid anymore. I'm every bit the legend that you are, except my legend is one that is handed down to the youngsters as positive, whereas your story was handed down to the players to turn them into slaves for dope and women! Young cats who wanted to "play like Charlie Parker" thought they had to stuff they veins full of filth to get there. You know, the first time I shot that shit was with the thought: "If it works for Bird, it works for me."

Bird: Good.

'Trane: Good?

Bird: Yeah, good. Bebop is a life of hardship, pain, a life in the streets. No one will ever play like Bird unless they experience the pain I felt just waking up in the morning. That pain is jazz, brother. Even you, even you needed that pain in the end. You escaped yours, I leaned into mine, but the pain is the truth that we can live by.

'Trane: You mean shooting so much junk that you don't have enough to feed your family? You mean getting so sick that you can't even get on stage without puking up the Italian sandwich

94

you ate for lunch? You mean being so desperate for junk that you allow yourself to get cheated by pimps and lowlives?

Bird: You're goddamned right that's what I mean. You see, jazz is all about the body man. Your horn is an extension of your body. You've got to *feel* your body first. That's what junk did for me, baby. When you're sick, you feel your body screaming at you. It's hollering for that junk. And when you shoot it, man, that junk feels so good, your body is floating. And when you're perfectly in tune with that body, the horn becomes its natural extension. That's how I created bebop.

'Trane: You see, I used to think like that. But I outgrew that. The horn isn't a part of your body man, it's a portal from this world to heaven. That's what it should be, anyways. Music can't be bogged down to just what's in front of us, it has to echo out into the cosmos! And how could I connect to the universal when I was stuck inside a club, in the streets, and in my body? How could I find *A Love Supreme* when I was so full of need for a drug that I wasn't even capable of thinking about anything else than my next fix? Music can't be selfish, man! You can't reach the sublime when you're a slave to addiction.

Bird: Music *is* selfish. And obsessive. God damn, that's all it is, self-centeredness! You complain about how you weren't able to love, well I gave up love in the pursuit of the music. I left Rebecca in Kansas City. I told her, "Sorry, I can't love you, I only love music and myself and you'll be better off without me." I made sure my mama took care of her and I moved on out. Junk made everything clearer. It crushed my self-doubt and dulled my guilt, and that's what I needed to be great. Clarity. Junk is like a consolidated loan, brother. All of life's problems melt into the only problem: dope. A great artist needs his life's problems simplified.

'Trane: But that life is never simple; it sure as hell wasn't when I was a junkie. I made a goddamn fool of myself! I had the best gig in the world, in Miles' band, in the band of the best trumpeter in the world! And I'd end up falling asleep and picking my nose on stage, looking like a fool!

Bird: Don't hold it against the drug that you couldn't handle. And sure, we all look goofy on drugs sometimes, that's part of the fun of it.

'Trane: There's nothing fun in sickness and selfishness. I was shooting drugs because I didn't feel right with myself, and with god. Because on stage. I didn't feel free to play what I was hearing in my head. Because I needed to dull that pain.

Bird: I never gave a fuck about any of that. You think I had time to feel pain? Fuck no, man! I practiced my head off, there was nothing else to do. And to keep practicing, I would drink, and I would shoot junk. I turned my body into a machine that could feel no pain. When the neighbors back in Kansas City would scream at me to stop the racket, I'd take my sax and my smack down to Paseo Park, and I'd shoot up and play all night. Just beautiful nights. Blowing my horn out to no one in particular.

'Trane: You know I saw you play in 1945 with Dizzy. I had never heard anything like it in my life. I had never heard a cat play double time, I thought playing like that was impossible.

Bird: And you think I ever would have played like that if I wasn't high as a kite and a mean, selfish bastard who only cared about music and the next fix?

'Trane: I think your talent was god given. Dizzy shunned hard drugs his whole life.

Bird: That's right, he's Dizzy, he ain't no Charlie Parker...he not even John Coltrane. We became what we are because we tasted the abyss. Art is self-degradation. And even though you got clean, it's that degradation that gave you perspective. It showed you truth. Let me ask you this, John: do you honestly think you would have made those masterpieces if you hadn't bottomed out? Would you have found the sublime if you hadn't gotten so sick that your body became a prison that you wanted to escape? Would you have experienced true beauty if you hadn't polluted yourself motherfucker?

'Trane: All that dope addiction did for me was delay. It locked me in stasis. I didn't get one iota better while I was using. I was stuck inside the confines of my own skill. I diverted to technique because I had no way to connect to the beyond.

Bird: But those drugs marked your spiritual rebirth my man – or whatever you want to call it. It's that yin and yang. You needed the dark to find the light. I found the light in jazz. And when I played on junk, I was yin and yang all at once.

'Trane: Perhaps you would have reached greater heights had you found the strength to kick junk. But we'll never know.

Bird: What, you think I should feel unsettled by what I achieved and what I did not? Is that what you're saying?

'Trane: What I'm saying is that, free of drugs, I found a new quality in jazz. That in modal jazz, you connect with an audience on a primordial, on a godly level. I learned that jazz was pure freedom. No longer was I playing what needed to be played to get paid and get my fix. I was opening myself to an energy that I could channel and share with an audience. Maybe I did need those strung-out years to find that, but I never would have found it if I kept burying my soul in junk until it killed me.

Bird: I'm supposed to act like you copying Ornette and playing at the Village Vanguard without a pianist required some godly intervention? Shit, I could have thought of that on a gram of dope and a ⅕ of whiskey! Bebop was perfection, and I found that perfection on dope. Shit, man. I'm fuckin' glad I croaked out before the 1960s came on... I don't think I could stomach all you cats pandering to white intellectuals with that free jazz bullshit.

'Trane: But what is music if not universal? Why should it not contain all the universe at once? Why should jazz not be open to every man, woman and child who is looking to connect with the spirits that tie us together?

Bird: Because that's all bullshit, baby! Jazz is the music of the streets. It's the sound of icy cool heroin flowing through the veins. It's the sound of damp, dark hotel rooms. It's the sound of violence and struggle. It's the sound of the here and the now.

'Trane: But jazz needs to evolve. It can't be in the here and now when it stagnates. This is what happened in our absence. It is now of little relevance to the world we left behind.

Bird: Maybe it had nowhere else to go. Maybe it was a moment specific to us and specific to the lives we lived. And from where I sit,

I'm fine with that. Jazz carried me through a fast and hard life, and that's all I needed from it. When me and Dizzy dropped "Now's the Time," the faggot journalists hated it. "Good," I thought. It's not for them. It's for me. But you John, you pandered. You made jazz a thing for hipsters to listen to in the lounges paid for by their mommy and daddy, way up in the tallest buildings of Greenwich Village. That's not me, that's not cool. That's a betrayal of the principles of our thing.

'Trane: You say betrayal, I say evolution. I say it was an *Ascension*. With a clean mind and soul, I — and some others, like Miles, Ornette, Dolphy, and other clean cats — established jazz as not just a music for clubs and lounges. But as a defining American art form of the century.

Bird: Bebop didn't need to become some goddamn perversion of itself to become that motherfucker. That's all your free jazz was – a god damned kink. And you know I've got nothing against kinks or vices. Pussy. Dope. Booze. I loved it all. I remember one time in the mid '40s, I was so dope sick at Hollywood Studios that I could barely find my reed. Someone gave me a handful of Benzedrine tabs, and I thought they were goofballs! Instead of satiating the sickness, they made it worse! All the demons of dope sickness wrapped around me and tightened around my throat, suffocating me like a pack of anacondas. But I played through that session with every ounce of energy I had left, and what I squawked was glorious! It almost killed me, and yet I was alive, playing as if my very survival depended on it! Jazz happens at the edge of life and death. No thought behind it. No artistic concept. It comes from the body. It comes when you can't think anymore, and you have to use every bit of your strength to stay on key. Man, that's bebop.

'Trane: And don't you ever worry that your notoriety may have overshadowed your contributions to our thing.

Bird: Why would I worry about that? Sure, I missed the time of records and albums and critical acclaim. I missed the '60s. But I know that time would never have come without me. I gave jazz a narrative by living life on my own terms. By simply being myself and doing what the fuck I wanted to do — slamming smack, fucking women, drinking whiskey, gobbling pills. Them white hipsters who made you rich did so because they wanted to buy a piece of the cool that came from me, like the sweat from my pores. Heroin is part of our legacy every bit as much as I am part of the legacy of jazz. Denying that is denying reality. All the best cats were junked out. All the best cats lived for music and getting high. I lived the way I lived and died on my own terms. And for all your handwringing, John, what did you get? Your clean lifestyle couldn't buy you but six more years than I got?

'Trane: I found inner peace. Death becomes a small thing when you felt the peace I felt.

Bird: Death got us no peace...If it did, then why the fuck we here? Fighting over our differences to no end? All that matters is living how you want to live. I wanted to live with music and drugs. And I did. I need nothing else. Maybe I missed this "inner peace" of yours, but I felt good. I felt good every damn day, and when I didn't I went out, made the hustle, and I got that feeling back any which way I could. That, my friend, is bebop living.

'Trane: I pray for you, Charlie.

And so it went, on and on, endlessly. The music kept playing. The styles kept clashing. And the cats kept bickering. There was no one truth. This thing, jazz, had no agreed upon definition. There's no beginning or ending here. And it's very seldom that anyone escapes.

CHAPTER 6

◆ letter ◆

Dear Phillip,

Your death haunts and threatens me. It's a spirit that visits me in my dreams and smiles with the most insidious intentions because it knows my truth. It taunts me. It knows that I'm a liar, and it laughs. Your death is a manifestation of all who wish to harm me, of all the harm that I have done and long to do to myself once more. Why won't you just leave me alone?

Your legacy is a most persistent reminder of sobriety's ephemeral nature, and its delusions. Your death transpired three months before my last shot of heroin. I feel linked to your ghost. It's hard for me to watch your films. Watching them frightens me. The 10 years that have gone by without a shot are shadowed by your end. Once a junkie, always a junkie. We both know what I'm talking about. It becomes a part of you. Years after its chemical debris has left the body, the drug lingers. Junk flickers in and out of reality; once forgotten, it comes back to remind you of the power it holds over you. It grasps you tight in its wings; its three heads whisper sweet nothings in your ear. Do you hear what I'm trying to say? We're separated by a mortal coil.

After *Capote* came out, you said something on *60 Minutes*. You looked good in the interview. You're a fat heaving fuck, as ever – but you look dignified. You have two-day stubble and well-parted thick hair glistening in that strawberry blonde. You're wearing glasses, and you seem to be playing the part of the humble thespian. It works. You radiate coy charisma. Steve Kroft hangs on your every word as you blush and smirk through your responses. And then, the broadcaster asks you about drugs. About how you got clean and the reason you stopped.

"I panicked," you reply. "I panicked because I had so much to do, and I wanted to do and accomplish things"

And then you did accomplish those things - probably beyond your wildest fantasies. Iconic performances. Awards. You are remembered as one of the most gifted actors of an entire generation. You are sorely missed. It wasn't enough though, was it? All the success, the glamour and the accolades – only briefly did they fill the emptiness that heroin once filled. All that money, the praise, all those cocktail parties with these beautiful, coked out social climbers telling you how wonderful you were, it wouldn't work, would it? That gaping hole at the center of your soul didn't go away. And at 47-years-old, the hole became a crater. Not even your children's love could fight it. You saw it. You felt it. You killed yourself to fill it once more. What happened? $1,200 worth of dope at once? A *lot* of fucking heroin. What were you thinking? I refuse to accept your choice to gamble everything away just to squirt some more dope into your arms. To do so would be to accept something incredibly painful about myself. That I understand you. That I feel connected to you. That this death could be my own.

You were the rarest of Hollywood actors. You brought the versatility and manic virtuosity of the character actor to leading roles and the magnetic presence of the leading man to supporting roles. All these other Hollywood actors now are repulsive to me. The decline of the movie star has coincided with the decline of American cinema and the process of artistic erosion that began at the turn of the 21st Century — when you were still on the rise, on your trip to replace misery and emptiness with art and success — has perhaps completed itself.

Nothing in your acting was forced, but it was disciplined. It was the product of an extreme dedication to self-excavation. What a contradiction. An unbearable burden. The key to your sublime talent was also the thing that made you vulnerable to the evils of life. This terrifies me.

The sincerity with which you approached the craft of acting and the art of cinema, your heart-wrenching intensity, feels like a faraway memory. Maybe you were always a ghost. Maybe you were the entity that infected the souls of the characters you played. Across all your performances, a palpable unease flowed through the beings you inhabited.

Your characters are the perfect embodiments of male anguish. Scotty's unrequited lust in *Boogie Nights*. Truman Capote's lurid fascination and lust for a killer destined to die. Lancaster Dodd, the man who thinks he is God but can't transcend his own worldly flaws. The multitudes of human complexity that you gave Lancaster go beyond a mere actor's duties. It was only you who could play this madman, this delusional neurotic who has convinced himself of his infallibility.

And what were the lies that you told yourself? Did you ever stop believing them? We need to hold onto our delusions. The facade that I've projected around me where I can hide my weaknesses is all that I have to protect me. Without this facade, the cracks that I've tried to pave over in my performance of a decent man will break open. We seek transcendence and thirst for divinity. You sought it in performance. And yet our passions for the earthly pleasure of blessed poppy threatens us with its seductive allure. Its memory never leaves. It never left you.

We both had the experiences that put us onto a path of life and death. Yours was witnessing a production of Arthur Miller's *All My Sons* when you were 12. Mine came from *Psychotic Reactions and Carburetor Dung*, a collection of Lester Bangs' best writing. Lester, the most brilliant rock n' roll critic of all time, was another character that you played. I would watch *Almost Famous* (a terrible film) again and again just to watch you bring Lester to life with the humor and charisma he deserved. Drugs killed Lester. Drugs killed you. Someday I will die. Nonexistence. How is it? For you, suffering and art were inextricably linked. You once said, "Acting is torturous, and it's torturous because you know it's a beautiful thing." Can beauty not spring forth from joy? It appears not. When anguish is the default position, we need to find relief. Art and beauty provide relief, but only for so long. The act of creation is suffering itself. To inject heroin is pure. It requires little more than the ritual. And unlike art, it's a ritual that is a pleasure unto itself, isn't it Phil?

You developed a sadomasochistic relationship with your work, it would seem. The more you suffered, the more *true* it seemed to become. Your greatest characters present themselves as stable and well put together only to hide a deep well of pain and discontent. The

106

normalcy they project falls apart under the slightest scrutiny (another aspect of your work that I painfully identify with). Your middle-class pain, the lonely boy from the broken home, is so banal as to be universal. I share this banality. But that doesn't make pain any less real now, does it? Maybe we are drawn towards the needle because our pain is tethered to an inescapable sense of failure. When you are brought up with advantage, the illusion of happiness is a fatal shot.

I can't help but wonder if the power of your performances is actually rooted in an utter lack of acting. You barely had to act because these characters were little more than pieces of your shattered soul. What did Solondz see in you that he saw in Allen? You hardly read as a lonely pervert (albeit, you do read as lonely). It's impossible to imagine you making predatory phone calls to women. These details are beside the point. Maybe it was the singular alienation you radiated that drew Solondz to you. Perhaps "artist" is the delusion that we carry to keep on going. The one we hold onto so that we stay alive. Maybe that delusion faded for you. It's bound to fade for all of us.

Sidney Lumet wasn't the flashiest director. He didn't have the exquisite violence of Scorsese, the genius of Kubrick, or the philosophy of Coppola. But Lumet understood cinema as storytelling better than anyone. He was a firm believer in the bare tools of filmmaking: actors, screenwriters, lighting men, cameramen, propmen. He was known for an uncanny talent for pitch perfect casting. When he cast someone, he believed there was no one else who could conceivably play that role.

I think of *Before the Devil Knows you're Dead* endlessly. It's a film of unmitigated tragedy; a story about the holes we bury ourselves in and the irreparable harm we do to ourselves. It's one of those late career masterpieces recognized only years after the passing of its director. On the surface, it's about two brothers. Hank (Ethan Hawke) is the perennial failure, hard up for cash to hold onto custody of his daughter. But Andy's plight (yours) is more sinister. To the world, he's a successful real estate broker married to a beautiful woman. But in private, he's a white-collar criminal whose heroin addiction has spiraled out of control. The two brothers plot to stage a robbery at their parents' jewelry store, hoping that their parents can collect the insurance pay out without anyone getting hurt. The robbery goes horribly, predictably wrong and their mother is killed. Both of the brothers unravel, but your unraveling Phil is so much darker. It's an unraveling that is near impossible to read as pure fiction. Lumet's late masterpiece now reads as a prophecy of your tragic demise.

When Andy approaches Hank to knock over their parents' store, the change in your character's demeanor is jarring. The smooth-talking businessman and loving husband is replaced by a frantic and anguished soul. Slowly, the tangled web of secrets that suffocate your character unfold and your portrayal of Andy's undoing is a nightmare that I've lived. When Andy stops at his dealer's apartment, memories of my own heroin-washed desperation are triggered. Sweating, fractured, disoriented, enraged, Andy manically rings the doorbell. Finally, a tiny, homosexual rent boy wearing nothing but a robe and a handgun stashed in his thong lets him in. In that scene, Andy's guilt becomes a force reflected in his chaotic body language; he rubs his temples, cracks his neck. The sickness of need is boiling beneath his skin. Your portrayal of addiction here is more realistic than anything I've ever seen. The rent boy comes in, takes his money, prepares a shot, and ties Andy off with a succulent dose of icy-hot heroin. Andy slumps back into a chair; the shot has eased his physical need but has barely dulled his psychological defeat and deep well of loneliness.

Andy's monologue doubles as a cry for help. I think you were crying out too.

The thing about real estate accounting is that you can, you can, add down the page or across the page and everything works out. Everyday, everything adds up. The, the total is always the sum of its parts. It's, uh, clean. It's clear. Neat, absolute. But my life, it, uh, it doesn't add up. It, uh... Nothing connects to anything else. It's, uh... I'm not, I'm not the sum of my parts. All my parts don't add up to one... to one me, I guess.

Your life ended up mirroring Andy's to a tragicomic degree. Your wife kicked you out of the house. Instead of doing what needed to be done to return to her and your children, you holed up in a West Village apartment. You dove into work. You did an off-Broadway production of Chekhov's *Ivanov*. They say that the play affected you deeply. But I know the truth Phil, I know the truth because it's a truth I know: nothing changed. That play didn't make you unhappy. The unhappiness never went away and the delusions that you clung to in order to suppress it were fading. The truth is that art couldn't save you. Performing couldn't save you.

I will cling to my delusions. I will do everything I can to believe my own delusions. You died to remind us that our sins will kill us. I hold no ill will towards you. But I reject your weakness.

Sincerely,
Adam Lehrer

◆ master fiend ◆

Prevel woke up stressed, while his wife Rolande and two small children slept. He had spent the evening trying to write in silence. The words would not come. He wasn't able to write in a single-minded and industrious way, but at the end of the night he had at least put some words on the paper. They were words of frustration and stasis. His was a poetry of the inability to write poetry. He needed new direction. His family's second floor walk-up was unusually peaceful in the small hours of the morning. Taking advantage of the stillness, Prevel smoked and violently coughed while hunched over his dinner table, his wrist cramping. The baby started crying at around 3am. He didn't get up, and toned out Rolande's pleas for his attention. Her rage shifted from his poor parenting towards his shameless philandering with the woman who lived downstairs. Avoiding a physical altercation, he went down to his mistress Jany's room.

Reaching for the cigarettes on his nightstand as a streak of light pierced through a crack in the window shades, he considered the difficulties of the day ahead. Jany, who was nude save for her panties, was holding her breasts, pushing them upwards. Her tangled blond locks, white and fair skin, the sinews that ran down the arch of her back and the drugs that deadened her mind - all this gave her an ethereal quality that the poet could not resist. She was Millais' *Ophelia* lost in the city. Prevel was aware that his desire for her was separate from love. He loved his wife, and he slept with her on occasion - but he *desired* Jany. He didn't understand why he couldn't have both. Artaud had nothing but love for Rolande, he respected her motherhood and her tenderness. He had warned him that Jany was an evil presence in his life, but Prevel didn't know what to make of it. Most people didn't understand that Artaud was an ardent moralist. Prevel often had to endure Artaud's screes against frivolous sexual promiscuity. Prevel cracked his neck, and finished the cigarette whilst looking out the window onto the bright sunlit streets of Saint-Germain-des-Prés.

Having to pick up Artaud made his mornings stressful. At the very least, it meant discomfort and inconvenience. He'd have to haggle with doctors and their stinginess with morphine, walking all around the city to get Artaud whatever he needed. But at the same time, he felt there was something noble in doing the old poet these favors. Artaud had told him early on that he needed "all the opium in Paris so that he could work." And Artaud was working at a ferocious rate. Prevel, in awe of him and suitably embarrassed by it, felt more purposeful supplying Artaud's highs than he did writing his own poetry. Artaud seemed genuinely enthusiastic about Prevel's work. That this was coming from a man who held masterpieces in contempt was a source of hope for Prevel. Since for Artaud art came from (and only from) the body - Prevel believed that he too could harness the requisite corporeal discomfort. But as he put on his black blazer over his rumpled white dress shirt, he remained uncertain.

Prevel left Jany's apartment without checking on his wife and children upstairs. That would only slow him down, so he left five francs under the door for them to eat – and so that he may assuage his conscience. The air outside was bitterly refreshing - good walking weather. Prevel had told Artaud that he'd have the drugs for him at around noon, which gave him an hour and 45 minutes to get to the pharmacy, hassle the pharmacist, and make the 45 minute trip to the Ivry-Sur-Seine. It was not always a convenient way to spend his days. Prevel thought himself less as a drug pusher and more as a facilitator of escapism, an essential component of Artaud's creative process. He wasn't his muse - he knew better than to self-aggrandize in such a vulgar way - but he did procure the element from which Artaud derived inspiration from.

Morphine, laudanum and opium were easier to get for Prevel than for Artaud, but it wasn't exactly easy either. As a psychiatric patient, Artaud wasn't legally able to purchase controlled substances. Prevel suffered routine humiliation as doctors grilled him with questions about his "ailments" and what his specific need for these drugs was. The neighborhood pharmacist stood behind the counter. His obscenely engorged frame was the width of the two fully stocked shelves behind him. His pre-diabetic breath was as putrid as a river in the early springtime. There was a whiff of the *Croix de feu* in this rotund tyrant's comportment. He demanded to be put in touch with Prevel's *généraliste* at the dispensary. This would be an unnecessary nuisance for Prevel as his doctor was in on the score – and in any case would be too blind drunk to answer the telephone. Losing his patience, Prevel eventually declared that he was happy to take his money elsewhere. The slug's eyes widened, his lips pursed as he huffed, and turning towards the shelves – grabbed two bottles of 10mg laudanum tincture and handed them across the counter to Prevel. As Prevel hopped off the train, he saw some labor protests outside the station. He found it amusing that Artaud, who was dismissive and contemptuous of such things, ended up in this communist stronghold. He seemed happiest amongst the things that made him unhappy; anger was what made him feel alive, it was what he survived on – pure antagonism, not mere contrarianism. Still, everyone was enraptured by him. Prevel himself was totally in his thrall. Even Artaud's greatest enemies and critics felt small in his presence. He filled every room with an air of menace and splendor.

As Prevel arrived at the hospital a chill ran down his spine. He always felt like this before meeting Artaud. As he approached the writer's room, he heard screaming and hissing behind the door:

the superiority of American products,
and the fruits of American sweat in all fields of activity
and of the superiority of the possible dynamism of force.
Because one must produce

Prevel thought he heard these words but couldn't tell in this noise…the sounds of a paranoiac demon worshipper whose power over reality was waning…or growing…a blend of abject weakness and unbridled strength. The strength was derived from this peculiar subjectivity; the weakness in that this subjectivity was irremediably embodied. The unity of these two competing forces brought his art to life.

It must have been less than a second after knocking on the door, when Artaud's skeletal head peeked through the window and looked over Prevel.

"Monsieur Prevel," Artaud said, "It's wonderful to see you. Please, enter, enter, of course!" Prevel smirked, and walked into Artaud's apartment. The apartment was sparsely furnished; just a small dining table with four chairs lining it, a mattress, an easel board and a wall of portraits. Across the floor were crumpled pages Artaud had written and frantically discarded. He wasted no time. Artaud wore a rumpled blazer jacket over an off-white fisherman sweater and a fashionable loose neck-tie. His hair, thinning back towards the middle of his scalp, was tousled. He was, not and forever, the image of the artist he created.

"Were you successful?"

Prevel nodded and handed Artaud the two bottles. Without hesitation, Artaud grabbed them and rushed them over to the kitchen table. He opened one tincture, inserted an eye dropper and sucked an alarming amount of the opiated fluid before dropping it directly onto his tongue. Artaud looked like a feral lizard with his tongue extended, manically focused on absorbing every drop of the acidic tasting drug.

In moments like these, Prevel had cause to contemplate the ways in which Artaud's body and appearance had radically mutated over the past twenty years. This was once a strikingly beautiful man. Artaud's body now looked deformed and depleted. His movements were fractured and tangled, like his joints had lost every flexibility. In a sense, Artaud's body had become a testament to the chaotic forces that flowed through him, subject to years and years of alchemical torture and occult experiments at the hands of some evil sorcerer. Artaud had been victimized by a beastly regime of electroshock therapy for years, a modern sorcery. His withered body now stood in testament to the liminal space between two worlds; through him we could see that which lies beyond. He was, like Aumvor the Undying, a necromancer who lived beyond his natural age by feeding on the souls of those around him. Artaud subsisted on the humiliation and degradation of his flock. He was animated by his own cruelty and their trauma. Physically, he looked dead. And yet, he lived.

Prevel was unsure if Artaud was even aware of the unseen magic that coursed through his being or if he knew the difference between the reality that they could both see and the one solely available to Artaud. Although, Prevel suspected, that his writing, his words, were his attempts to give it some definable form. Being subject to these forces left Artaud looking like a Giacometti figure, attenuated and suffering. When you looked at Artaud in this manner, Prevel thought, his need for opium was glaringly apparent. His aim was for the body to transcend itself, but the body was fragile and transcendence exerted a supernatural stress upon it. In opium, Artaud found a substance that kept him temporarily whole whilst caught between two worlds.

Prevel sat across the table from Artaud, who was slinking back into his chair as the relief washed away the sickness in his body. Prevel realized that after all these afternoon rituals together, he had never once seen Artaud nod out in the way that junkies have a tendency to. Nor had he seen him appear noticeably high. For one, Artaud's innate "strangeness" — his deific quality — would have made it hard for the onlooker to distinguish between his sobriety and intoxication, but Prevel thought it was also something else. Artaud told him that he needed, not wanted, but *needed* these drugs — and Prevel believed him. When the opium took effect, Artaud's soul wormed its way back into his body. If the transcendental was Artaud's natural habitat, opium was his way of reentering the body. Without the drug, Artaud might have never gotten a word on the page. The opium was like a sealant; it briefly trapped Artaud in his corporeal form so that he could transmute the

116

energy of beyond back through his body and onto the page. In this regard, Prevel thought, we owe opium a great deal. Getting Artaud his fix was heroic work, and this made Prevel happy.

"Thank you for this. Would you care for something?"

Prevel nodded. "Some coffee would be pleasant."

Artaud got up and attended to the coffee. Prevel waited eagerly for Artaud to start sermonizing. He felt that Artaud's raw language, his conversational prose, was more insightful than his writing. Something was always lost when Artaud was forced to transmit energies through the written word, like they were dulled with every passing moment that they remained trapped in his mind. Drugs and conversation, though, made him into a transmitter to the gods. The idea emerged in his head like it was sent from beyond and then immediately released through his mouth. But the longer he held onto that idea, like during writing, the longer the idea eroded. In conversation, Artaud was unadulterated by art and literature.

"You know, Prevel," said Artaud, "I must do all the work that I can now, before the pornographer doctor zaps me to steal my power and I no longer exist."

"Which doctor is this?"

"Ferdiére. I would like to strangle him, to feel his soul exit his body so I can devour it, before ripping open his dead insides and throwing them against the wall. There are people who wish to do me great harm, but they don't know what I am capable of."

Prevel considered this for a moment. Artaud poured him a cup of coffee, to which Prevel added two sugar cubes. Artaud drank more opium and closed his beady eyes, slumping back into his chair. Prevel looked over Artaud's drawings, many of which were completed while Artaud was under Ferdiére at the Rodez mental institution.

"Have you been drawing at all lately?" asked Prevel.

"My drawings are spells that I cast upon my subjects. They are revenge. Revenge against the evil people that are trying to destroy me. They'll destroy you too, Jacques!" He screamed the last sentence with his fists clenched and chest raised up.

Artaud took periodic sips of the laudanum throughout the conversation, he didn't use opium like most people did. The average opium user dosed, enjoyed the dose, and then waited until it wore off to take another one. Artaud dosed repeatedly until the bottle was gone, never demonstrating signs of intoxication. He enjoyed opium like most people enjoyed water. It hydrated him. Nourished him. It was impossible to tell if the drug was making him higher or more lucid. Prevel was perplexed by Artaud's excess, knowing this meant more future procurement errands.

Artaud was almost always in a state of prophetic paranoia, declaring the destruction of his enemies while scratching his nose, or screaming to the heavens about all the myriad ways they have wronged him. Prevel, in all truth, tired of Artaud quickly, because it was exhausting to be so deeply in his thrall. He could never tell what took precedence in Artaud's association with him; his literary worth or the drugs he brought him. Before getting up to politely make his exit, Artaud stopped Prevel by putting his palm to his chest.

"Let's go for a walk. If I don't walk it's possible that my enemies will unleash the demons upon my soul, or what's left of it."

Prevel, knowing he hadn't much choice in the matter, stood up to put his pea coat back on. Artaud took one gulping swig of laudanum, and then violently shook his head with a feral glee as the harsh fluid stuck to his tongue. Artaud, in his crumpled dirty overcoat reminded Prevel of a lonesome scarecrow, perfectly still yet full of terrifying potential. Walking along, he'd chain smoke while Artaud dallied. He'd take about 10 steps, stop, tilt his head like a wild mongoose, and make some macabre observation about the state of humanity or a paranoid accusation about his perceived enemies. Across the courtyard Prevel and Artaud walked through, there were children playing hopscotch. Artaud was displeased.

"Every child born is a knife in the belly of my lifeless body," he said. "All sexual intercourse is an attempt to drain me of my power. This is clear to me. But perhaps there should be an Artaud baby, to protect my essence."

Prevel, by now accustomed to overlook the occasional bizarre statements, listened intently to this remark. If he could annotate everything that Artaud said, he'd have material for a powerful work indeed.

They stopped at a picnic table in an unusually lush patch of greenery sealed away from the city. Despite how volatile Artaud must have seemed to most people, especially after decades spent in mental institutions, Prevel felt comfortable around him. They had now been cavorting for a year, since Artaud's release from Rodez in 1946. And although their friendship must have appeared peculiar to onlookers, the two men shared am unhappy bond. Prevel, suffering a horrific cough that he knew in his bones spelled doom, had lived a life of artistic rejection and failure. Artaud too felt slighted. His expulsion from the Surrealists had prefigured his subsequent banishment from polite society. Artaud believed that his madness fulfilled the Surrealist promise, the ultimate conclusion of which could only be to suffer at the hands of the state.

"When did you start using the opium," Prevel asked, emboldened by his curiosity after all this time.

Artaud huffed, hacked, and spat a thick membrane of mucus onto the grass. For a man who could never stop talking, he hated being addressed directly.

"The poet, the artist, Monsieur, is all too aware of the decay of his own body. His body is a dying matter, a husk of death, and he knows this all too well. Quite simply, Prevel, if I had not discovered opium, I would have been compelled to commit suicide. It was suicide or it was opium, that was the choice I was given."

Prevel had used all manner of opium, heroin, and laudanum, but he never ascribed it the importance that Artaud did. It made him feel pleasant, but it was nothing like what Artaud was describing. For Artaud, it was a sacrament. To consume opium is to thwart death.

"Haven't you ever wondered what it would be like to stop?"
"Damn you!" he exclaimed, standing up and gesticulating wildly. "Do you not listen? I told you, opium is life, not death! Without opium I would be resigned to oblivion, an oblivion of blackness, but with opium I can inhabit *this* oblivion, the oblivion of the living!"

120

"All the secret agencies, all these centers of power that seek to control the flow of opium to Artaud! They deny me the right to opium because they want me dead! They want me to cross over to the black in the hospital, that's why the hospital wouldn't give me opium! I had to wait them out or I would die, and the only reason I waited them out was so I could have opium once more and communicate the darkness that beckons me back and spews me forth! Let Artaud self-destruct, because destruction is an act of life, and opium is the piece that puts me back together again. You see, Prevel, I exist in all space and all time at once. Most people have one place, one dimension, and they are at peace. But the walls between realities crack around me. Opium is the sealant. Without it, I simply deteriorate into nothingness. Do you understand what I am telling you?"

Prevel nodded. He did understand, perhaps even more than Artaud realized.

"Do you prefer that I not work? Because that's what you ask of me when you ask me to not use opium. Coleridge used the opium, but he lived in shame of it, can you imagine? Being taught to feel shame about the thing that gives you life? Coleridge found the substance that allowed him to be engulfed in the darkness and the occulted forces of the universe and come back unharmed and communicate the devilish things he saw, and he rewarded himself with shame. He was a coward, and from beyond the grave he tries to destroy me! I can't be destroyed you see, because I have opium, and when I die I will be indestructible because while I lived I feasted on the alchemical tonic of tranquility itself! Coleridge wasn't killed by opium, he died of shame! And I have no shame about my power, or the force from which my power is harnessed. Artaud

121

is immortal, opium is power, and my enemies will feel the razor's edge of my sword as I hack deeper and deeper into their souls!"

Artaud put a few more droplets of the drug onto his tongue. He told stories. He spoke of the men that he'd killed. The women that wished him killed. He spoke of the secret knowledge that only he had access to, and boasted that only he and never Prevel would hold it. He told Prevel that a day would come when they clash, and they'd fight to the death. But that they'd do so respectfully, as men, slaves to an ocean of time.

"I'm getting a bit chilly" said Artaud, clenching his stick thin arms together across his chest.

"Let's go" Prevel said, "We can pay a visit to the junk doctor in Sur de Seine."

Artaud's eyes lit up at the suggestion.

CHAPTER 8

⋆ lost sessions ⋆

Ol' Dirty Drives to Houston

I just crossed over into Texas driving on the I-10. I've been driving straight since I stopped for the night in Philly. A long motherfucking drive. I'm in a 1997 Camry that was lent to me. Well, I took his keys from his nightstand and drove off. I feel uncomfortable, my stomach is fat as a fucking pancake. My ass is sweaty and itchy but it's too cold to turn the damn heat off. The only possessions I got with me are the golden velour sweatsuit I'm wearing, my Glock 19, and a hefty stash: an eightball of coke, some packets of Dust, an ounce of green and lots and lots of pills. I got Tramadol, I got Percodan, word. I got this new shit they callin' OxyContin. And I stop every hour to swallow more of them motherfuckers. I stop at the truck stops to snort the coke. The Four Tops is on the radio. "If I Were a Carpenter." These songs always make me think about the ol' days. About my mom's. Make me happy, but a little sad too. I'm on the run. They'll catch me eventually. I feel so confused that everything is clear. My heart is pounding and my mind is racing. The desert around me is pure black; all I see is the light of the road in front of me. How the fuck did I get here?

You got here because you're a failure. You were always going to fail, you fat fuck up. Only broke ass from the Fort that got the chances you got. And now look at you. Busted out of jail and driving to Houston to cut tracks with some fat bastard who makes rap slow?

I slap my face. Got to keep focused. Look ahead, look in front of you, at the light. Keep moving. Word. Everyone is trying to take my freedom. Or kill me. The cops done shot me. The hood done shot me. Da Clan feel less like a family every day. Word. The year 2000 almost over. A New Millennium, but everything seems old. I feel old. My life, exactly the same as it was, but worse. Word. I'm feeling fuzzy and I'm hearing voices. I chew on another one of they oxies and wash it back with a Coke, swishing it in my mouth and washing out that sour, medicinal flavor. I feel disrespected. I feel angry. Angry at RZA. Angry at the Wu Tang Clan. Angry at my legal problems, my money problems. Angry at myself.

I'm angry at the music press who treat me like I'm some kinda circus act. I never had the hatred for whitey that some of the brothers had. I grew up around broke folks. White, black. Didn't matter. Broke is broke. Not like them poor white folks was making me broke. I never felt real racism until I became a star. They don't get me, they don't see the art in what I do. How come when some cracker goes up on a stage and starts jacking his dick off he's called a genius and praised right there as an artist that the world needs to take serious. But when I do something crazy, shit − when ODB does anything, I'm called a lunatic, a thug, or whatever else they wanna call me. Welfare queen. Word. When I take MTV to collect a welfare check, I'm a low life. When I go on stage to steal Puff's Grammy and make a big scene, I'm unhinged or on drugs. I mean, I was on drugs, but so what? They just refuse to see the art in

126

what I do. They don't let a black artist be transgressive. That's the real racism right there. A white boy acts crazy and he's a genius.

Ol' Dirty acts crazy, and he's just crazy. But I dunno anymore. Maybe they right. My thoughts ain't so clear no more. I've always claimed to be of the Five Percent. But maybe I'm another brotha in the 85. I'm so lost. Word.

I'm a fugitive. I just busted out of rehab. Court mandated. Fuck it, it wasn't helping me none. I'm higher now than I ever was. They gonna put me in jail the first chance they get anyways, so might as well enjoy this while I'm out. Cut tracks. Make money. Provide for my family. Get bitches. Get high. Keep going.

How long you think this can go on? You got kids! A lot of kids! You gonna be leaving them without a pot to piss in at this rate!

I pull over to the side of the road outside Dallas for a second. I got very little left to lose. I gotta go back to jail, I can barely communicate this ocean of language inside my head. Word. I'm done pretending. But there's freedom in that loss of control. Word. I feel freedom. I feel like I can try something new, on my own. Who needs the rest of the Clan? Not me. I know I'm the rawest. Word. There ain't no one else that can do what I do. That brings what I bring. I can see Dallas in the rearview mirror. It looks pretty. Lots of lights. Everything looks pretty in the rearview.

You one dumb motherfucker son! How long you think this will go on? You're pissing it all away. You fucked it all up.

Word. I take a snort of coke, pop some more pills. These pills, these painkillers, they keep me steady. Nothing else works. I think I was always crazy. And sometimes I don't know if it's the crazy that made Ol' Dirty Bastard, or being Ol' Dirty Bastard made me crazy. They say I'm bipolar. Up and down. Word.

Well, cocaine gets me up. These pills keep me down. What's so bad about that? I light a menthol, roll the window down, and exhale that minty smoke out the car. Time to straight shoot it to Houston. Word. Maybe this will work out. It makes sense enough. Screw wants to work with a big rapper from New York. I want to see what's goin' on with these boys down south. Word. I get back on the road and step on the pedal a bit. Shit. Gonna keep it going while I'm still out here. Aight. Let's go get "screwed." I been screwed a long a while now anyways. Word.

DJ Screw Awaits a Felon on the Run

I've been up for three nights now. I feel bad, you know what I'm saying? It's Halloween. Unseasonably hot out here. Hotter than a motherfucker. I'm out on my front yard here on Fuqua Street, sitting on an Adirondack chair. Soaking up the sun. I'm too fat for this chair, I feel uncomfortable. I don't like the way that I'm so conscious of my body. I think about my stomach, seeping over my Dickie's shorts. It just don't feel right. Shit. You know what I mean?

I've already got the sweat dripping from my pores. I got the shivers. I'm getting those hot flashes, and my body achin' to the point where I can't even make a fist. That's always how I know it's coming on.

I squeeze my fist together a few times, and if my hand feels weak, I know I better get down to business. I go back into the crib, air conditioning washing over me, and head to the kitchen. From the refrigerator, I grab a two liter of grape soda and an ounce of that sizzurp. I don't drink coffee. As I mix it in the red plastic cup by my counter, looking through my window out the back yard, I feel a real kind of thrill all over me. Every time. I love mixing the shit like I love mixing the tracks. I grab my ounce of green out the silverware drawer and roll it up in a blunt. I walk back out to the front door.

Back on the lawn now, it's about 12 pm. The sun bakes on my skin. I take the first sip of the sizzurp, and my entire energy shifts. I down the cup in three more swigs. I close my eyes and let the chills dissipate. I can make a fist again, and there's a little pleasant scratch in my face. I feel something in me slowing down, like my insides are eating themselves. No one told me a fuckin' drink can lead to this kind of physical wreckage, know what I mean? No one ever tells you that your lifestyle and the culture you helped spawn could be the things that kill you. I feel closer to death every fuckin' day. Sure, we all headin' towards death. But I really feel it. It's close. It's breathing down my fuckin' neck. I open my eyes, and I breathe in deep. I grab the blunt and the lighter off the little picnic table next to my chair. I spark it, and breathe it down my charcoal lungs. I cough and wheeze when I exhale, feel the water dripping behind my eyelids. And I keep smoking it. I smoke half the blunt. Most of my niggas only need a couple hits to get to where they going. I need the whole blunt. Or at least most of it. It makes the lean a bit trippier. Makes the music sound a bit better. Makes life a little bit easier.

I breathe in the Houston air. It smells like sewage, gasoline, and gunfire. The smell is comforting. Know what I mean? I never venture outside this city. Can't remember the last time that I did. I see all these rappers traveling the world. They big stars now. But us Houston niggas, we stay here. We just want to rule our own city. But something in me burning. There's just no more way for me to deny my situation. I'm hooked on the sizzurp. I'm a fucking drug addict, brah. I'm not afraid of death, I'm afraid of dying too young. I need to do something, anything, different. I can't just be the guy producing raps slow my whole life. I mean shit, my raps will always be slow, but why can't the slow raps producer be as important as the RZA or Dre? Why can't I be like those motherfuckers? I got every bit as much vision as they do, and shit, I bet I got more heart. I got more soul in me because I know who I am, and I know where I'm from. I created a whole fuckin culture in this city, and I need the world to know that now. Re-lighting the blunt, I check my pager that's strapped to my belt buckle. Dirty says he'll be here in four hours. That crazy motherfucker drove here through the night to come record. He's on the run from the law. Sure, I invited him here because of the inevitable PR scandal. I can see it now: "Ol' Dirty Bastard Busts Out of Jail and Drives to Houston, Records with Local Legend DJ Screw." That's what's up, know what I mean? But I feel like me and Dirty will vibe. We both regular. We both from the hood. And we both get high. Who knows? Maybe this will be good. Maybe it's the start of something new. Know what I mean?

I gotta get out of this heat. I walk back inside and pour myself a 7/11 Big Gulp full of lean and grape soda. I sip it through a twisty straw as I walk to the back of my crib. My studio is my cave. It's like that cave where Superman goes. To think. But I can't think anymore unless I got the juice in me. The carpet in here is one of those psychedelic patterns, in these kinds of tan colors. It looks vintage and shit. There are two turntables on a desk in-between two stereo systems, makes the shit bang. On the other side of the room are racks of records. I got all the shit. My old favorites like BB King and James Brown. Plus, we got records and tapes by the whole Screw Crew. E.S.G. Lip' Flip. Trae. Z-Ro. Fat Pat. Fat Pat been dead and gone two years now. Went to go collect a fee from some snakey promoter's house and gets shot right outside the apartment. Right on South Drive. The promoter weren't even home. Can you believe that shit?

I chug the rest of the lean, and belch. The carbonation is laced with a hint of medicinal under flavor, which I've come to find pleasurable over the years. Lean burps, I sit back in my chair with an old Otis Redding record, "Spinning," and my eyes are pure water as I suck down another blunt. I'm down as fuck right now, but I ain't even phased by it. I love life to be slowwww. I need that warm feeling, that cushion of relaxation. Most people would be falling asleep right now, but me? I'm good. I slump back in the chair, and space out on a screwed version I did of "Pain in my Heart."

I was never involved with the gang life. A good kid. I love music, it's all I ever loved. But I can't be known forever as the fat producer from Houston that made raps slow, that shit sound gimmicky, know what I mean? When Fat Pat got shot, that nigga was about to be finishing his debut album. *Ghetto Dreams* it was called. Lot of industry heads was saying it'd be the first Houston record to go big time. Go national. But when he got shot, there was no rapper to promote the record. It fizzled out. I wasn't close with Pat, but his death shook me. I think it was… It was that I thought his success would be our success. The whole Screw Crew. I thought it would make me as a producer and as an artist. I thought I would be recognized not just as some afterthought. When he died, my dream died with it. And with nothing else to dream, I just drank more and more and more. It was like I was drinking to the end of it all. That's where I'm at now. Ain't no one gonna shoot me. I kill myself easy enough. I just need to do one thing big. Something everyone everywhere will remember.

The phone's ringing.

"This Screwed Up Records…"

"It's Dirty, I'll be there soon, we gonna' have to do this quick…"

I hang up the phone and head back to the kitchen to pour myself another cup. I have to get in the zone.

Ol' Dirty Bastard Approaches Houston

Damn, Houston hotter than a motherfucker. It's damn near winter and there's barely a breeze. But I keep the windows down always, I don't like air conditioning. I need the windows open or it gets too quiet. Can't deal with the quiet. It's 4 pm. Been driving for, fuck, a day or so. Word. It sorta look like LA except there ain't no water. It look like a city out of place, like its people want it to be something that it's not. Maybe that's why it's got a scene going on. All these rappers trying to put this place on the map. Maybe real hip-hop ain't just driven by the need to be recognized for your own self, but for your home to be recognized. I like that. Word.

Houston got some kind of vibe though. I'll give it that. It's got a lot of ambition. It's got character. Downtown real pretty and kept nice,

132

and these neighborhoods I'm driving through are colorful. Even the poor here must have pride in themselves. An aspiration of beauty. *What the fuck do you know about pride you insane, alcoholic, about to be incarcerated and mentally incapacitated motherfucker?*

There's a block of poor houses with the exact same shape, but every single one has its own unique color. It's different from Brooklyn, where you can tell the projects from a mile away. I'm wired as fuck. My eyelids are tweaking. I need to even out. I reach into my glove compartment and reach for the bottle of Percodan. I untwist the cap and drop three pills, 20mg a piece, into my mouth. I chew on them and don't even mind the chalky, astringent flavor. I don't care about taste no more. When you do enough drugs taste and shit like that doesn't matter. I gotta straighten myself out and it don't matter the taste. I wash the pill powder back with another can of Olde English. The best thing about these pills is they keep me sharp. When I drink and smoke crack I go into psychosis. Word. I done a lot of things I wished I hadn't just drinking and snorting cocaine or smoking crack. But these pills keep me sharp. Keep me clear. They take the edge off, and for someone like me, taking the edge off is about the best I can expect. I just gotta avoid the green – makes me paranoid. Word. Can't have that. I'm still on the run. Can't be worried about that. I realize that I've been swerving all over the road. I decide to pull into a gas station to call Screw and let him know that I'll be pulling up.

I pull into a station and it looks like one of those west coast gas stations you see in the movies. It's bright and colorful but it makes me feel lonely. I haven't talked to Shaquita in a long fucking time. I haven't seen my kids in a long fucking time. Shaquita says I need to clean myself up if I'm gonna be a father. She says I need to stop fucking around on her if I'm gonna be her husband. I don't know why I can't be different things to different people. There's many layers to me. There's many truths of Osiris. Osiris is the god of sex, of death, of resurrection, of all kinds of shit. I got so much in me. I can love my wife and my kids but sometimes I need to love other bitches too. I need to let myself go if I'm going to bring myself back. I see no contradictions here and I don't understand why people these days don't allow men to be men. I grew up in broke ass poverty and rose up to be one of the best in the world. The most original to ever do it. Ain't no father to my style. And now that I achieved my dreams, I can't enjoy the spoils of my victory? Fuck that. Word. No one is one thing. I'm many things. ODB, baby, is everything. Word.

Is this what we're telling ourselves, now? That we everything? That we got no responsibility to anyone? Man, you hardly anything. You NOTHING.

I pull up to the tank. I give the mans there my credit card. He looks hood. He's big, thick necked, with teardrops tattooed beneath his eyeballs – and other jail tats running up his arms. He's got a shaved head and stands at about 6 ft 3. He comes up to tell me my money no good here. I tell him nah nah. I pay for my gas. He appreciates. He respects it for real. Word. I refuse to leave the hood behind. Osiris might be a god, ODB might be a star, but Russell Jones just a man with a whole lot of problems. Problems like any man has. I tell him to fill the tank and to grab me a case of beer. Any kind of beer, I say, 12 pack. I put some loose change in the payphone to call the Screw man.

He answers:

"Yeah?"

"Yeah, it's Dirty, I'll be there in about 15 minutes. You got the studio ready?"

"Yeah, man, we good to go, everything racked up. You know what I mean?"

Word.

DJ Screw waits for Ol' Dirty Bastard to Roll Up On his Lawn

When Dirty's second call came through, I woke up from a slumber. I finished off three more cups of lean while hanging here in the studio. I was listening to the *Supafly* soundtrack and must have passed out while smoking a blunt. I never 'screwed' Mayfield before. Not sure why. Maybe I love him too much and think it's disrespectful or some shit. Know what I mean?

Screwing is an act of love, but also an act of hubris. It takes some moxy to slow down one of the greats and claim to make it better. Know what I mean? I've totally lost my sense of time, so I end up looking at my Rolex every few minutes. It takes me a while to get out of my chair. I'm dizzy. My eyes are so pinned I can barely see more than two feet ahead of me. I take a sip of water from a glass I left on the table and apply Visine to my eyeballs. I slap my cheeks, two-day stubble scraping the palms of my hands, and walk back out through the kitchen and the living room and out the front door. The sun is baking, so I sit on the front steps. In as much shade as I can catch. I used to love the heat. I'm so uncomfortable in my body, I can feel the clogging of my own arteries. I lose breath sitting down. And the lean only does so much now. It eases the unease, but it never takes it away entirely. In my gut I still doubt that Dirty is going to show up but he says he's almost here. I'll wait outside 15 minutes before he gets here. I rolled up a blunt to welcome him with. Figure he'll appreciate the gesture. Still no luck. He's not here. I'm having trouble keeping my eyes open. The haze of the heat coming off the landscape before me — the road, the colorful houses, the towering cities in the horizon — looks like a hallucinatory field. But that's all normal to me. I don't remember feeling any other way. I feel like I'm half alive. It's all become so routine. A beep of a car horn goes off. I think it's Dirty.

Dirty pulls up in a rented Camry. It looks like he got in a fender bender at some point during his journey, his right head light is smashed off. He really IS a crazy motherfucker. Broken parole and driving cross country in a busted-up rental that he most definitely can't return. He pulls up in the driveway, half the fuckin' car on the grass and the other half on the pavement. He emerges out of his car. He looks like hell, like he's running on something other than blood. But he's got a smile a mile wide.

Ol' Dirty Bastard Arrives At DJ Screw's Home Studio

I'm swerving all over the fuckin' road. It says his home was only three miles away but these stop lights are endless. My heart is beating out of control from a rock I smoked back at the station. The big gas man didn't seem to mind. The pills haven't hit me so I'm spun out, drinking a beer to soothe the edge. Shit. I'm feeling excited. It's good to try new shit. All right, here we go. Word. Green Stone. That's

Screw's street. He says it's a little white house. One floor. Broke motherfucker shit. Hood shit. My kind of shit. Man, they keep it real out here in Texas. No Suge Knight turning motherfuckers on each other for profit. No Biggies and Tupacs hating each other to feed the beast of controversy for they bloodthirsty fans. Nah, these Houston boys got nothing but love. Nothing but love. For the music. For the culture. For their city. Shit, I could get used to this. Word.

Must be hard for you to be around people who still have pride in themselves and where they come from.

Fuck, gotta snap out of it. Oh, fuck! I think that's the house. Yeah, that's it. That's Screw! I cut into the driveway real fast, too excited to hit the break immediately. I pull up. Screw walks up. Oh man, this motherfucker is nothing but love. I get out of the car. My god, Screw fatter than a motherfucker. He a fat stumpy little fuck. I thought they said he was in his 20s but he looks way older than that. Agh well. It's nothing but love, word.

"Damn Screw, I just drove 18 hours straight to come get here with you, God! It's good to be here, man. For real. Word." I give Screw a big-time hug. He wasn't expecting it.

"Oh, Dirty man, this an honor! We don't get many legends down here in Houston! We gonna put this motherfucker on the map with this shit!" says Screw.

"Aight, baby, let's do it. Show me the way."

"You sure you don't need to rest for a while? That was a long drive?" asks Screw.

"I'll rest when I'm dead, I'm good. I'm ready. I got rhymes, you got tracks, let's get in the lab."

"Aight, baby, well I got a gift for you…"

Screw pulls out a blunt. I don't wanna tell him it makes me paranoid and with my cocaine psychosis and opiate abuse it might cause me to have a full god damned freak out. I don't need to be buggin' right now. Word. But I thank him. And when he lights up, I take a hit. I caught my head off when I exhale and go to the glove compartment to grab my pills and my rock. When he sees what I'm doing he says, "Bring that shit if you want but I got the real good shit inside." I like this brother.

Ol' Dirty Bastard and DJ Screw Lay Down Some Tracks

Screw gave Dirty the tour of his house. Through most of its modest corridors, it was an ordinary, working class, southwestern home. The recording space looked like the living room of a white hippie college student, with its eastern-influenced rug and wooden walls and floors – but in its adornments it functioned as a shrine to hip-hop. Its walls were littered in posters for some of the greats. Eazy-E. C-BO. Lots of Houston local celebrities. There was not much mention of either Wu Tang Clan or the East Coast. But Dirty didn't mind, he was so paranoid he would have probably assumed that Screw hung Wu Tang posters to pander. His equipment was decent too, if not exactly the state-of-the-art shit RZA used since *Wu Tang Forever*.

Screw had an E-mu SP-1200, a Technics SL-1200MK2 Turntable, and an Alesis ADAT "Black Face." It reminded Dirty of the old days, when RZA was planning on World Domination with a sampler and a couple turntables. Dirty believed hip-hop should be, well... dirty. It had to be a music that represented where it came from. It had to embody the streets and the hard livin' they frame. It had to evoke petty crime and hustlin'. Drug addiction and poverty. Sleaze and menace. Hip-hop's turn towards entertainment worried Dirty, for sure, but what worried him more was that he would have no place within it if that turn was final. The fact that RZA was so intent on cleaning up the Wu Tang sound made Dirty feel ever more disconnected from the Clan. As Dirty was lost in thought, he reached into his pocket to rattle out some more pain pills. But just before he could take one, Screw stopped him.

"Save your shit," said Screw. "I got something that'll really knock your ass out."

Screw directed Dirty back to the kitchen and opened the refrigerator. There was almost no food in it at all. Instead, there were several stacked cases of Miller High Life. On the rack above the beer were six two-liter bottles of soda. Half of them were off-brand orange. The other half were the same off-brand grape. On the rack above the soda were medicinal bottles. In each bottle was a pint of codeine-promethazine. Screw grabbed two out of the fridge and asked Dirty his soda preference.

"Orange," said Dirty.

"See this, this the purple drink," said Screw. "This the codeine-promethazine. The sizzurp. The lean. This shit right here is the sound of DJ Screw. And the sound of DJ Screw is the sound of a whole city. The lean is the whole culture, my brotha."

Dirty, who felt like he could crawl out of his own body just to escape the agony of his cocaine withdrawal and had the sensation of bugs crawling up and down the insides of his arms, liked that idea. "Hell yeah, nigga. Mix me up with some of that shit. Word."

As Screw mixed the drink, Dirty walked a circle around the kitchen. He looked up at Screw and noticed a look of intense fascination in the producer's eyes as the liquids mixed together in the styrofoam cups.

"You look like some kind of mad scientist or something," said Dirty, "Your eyes light up with that shit."

"Well my brotha," replied Screw, "You'll see why real soon. I'm a little jealous that you get to try this shit for the first time. I need about four cups these days just to drink the sweats off."

"Shit, I heard that."

Screw handed Dirty a cup.

"Cheers, motherfucker, and welcome to Houston!"

"Cheers!"

Screw finished the entire cup in one drink. Dirty had trouble with the acidic sweet flavor at first but got over it. As they walked back to the studio, a beautiful surge of warmth and comfort enveloped Dirty's entire being. The cocaine psychosis vanished without a trace. All the paranoia he felt for years, now melted away. He didn't think about the cops that were on his ass, the wife and kids he left at home, the bitches ragging his ass for more child support, or the neighborhood brothas that were constantly trying to rob and kill him. He was in a new kind of zone, this purple drink really was an elixir. Screw didn't look good. He was stumbling, and his eyes were periodically fluttering backwards into his skull. Dirty had seen lots of rappers get carried away on booze, coke, crack, and pills. But he'd never seen an industry nigga that looked this weathered. Screw looked exhausted, like his body was shutting down. His movements were slow, whereas Dirty always moved fast. He couldn't ever stop moving, because to cease movement was to let people see through the performance.

"So what you got for me God, what am I spitting over?"

"I got some tracks that I've been working on, a little psychedelic like, I think they'll bring something out in Osiris that maybe the RZA even couldn't. Lot of heads in this scene have shark bit my style, man. But it ain't a screw tape unless I screwed it. Nevertheless, I want to push this shit farther. I want this to be special, something I might be remembered by, know what I mean? I don't have much more time."

Dirty, who was nodding himself now, was unnerved by Screw's statement about not having time. But he understood the sentiment.

"Awright, god. Play it," said Dirty.

Screw put a self-produced track on the turntable. At first, it didn't sound quite unlike the tracks he'd been self-releasing for a decade now, some of which Dirty had heard and admired. But it didn't sound breathtaking or anything. But as Dirty downed his cup of lean, and its serenity covered the world with a translucent glow, he started to hear something special. This wasn't just slow hip-hop beats, it was musical hypnosis. It isolated the funkiest part of a track and stretched it out until it became a blurred hum of transcendent beauty. Dirty could hear some of the samples that the producer used. Samples of Four Tops. The Comrads. Digital Underground. Dirty was pleased.

"So what you think?" asked Screw.

"I can vibe with this shit, let's get it going."

A sensation or relief washed over Screw, who hadn't realized how nervous he'd been up until that point. He was too leaned out to even notice his own anxiety. But he was smiling big now. He couldn't believe it. A big New York rapper that wanted to record with him.

"All right baby, get in the booth, you want another cup?" asked Screw.

"Yeah, another cup of that lean. But also need something to get a little wild, you mind if I smoke a rock or two? Do what you got to," said Screw. "But I prefer wet, you smoke that?"

"You got any?"

"Hell yeah!"

Screw prepared a blunt and sprinkled a bit of PCP in before twisting it. He lit up and his pupils dilated instantly. It felt like the stimulation of the lean was at the bottom of an opioid hole it was furiously climbing out of. The counteracting effects of the two drugs never ceased to be thrilling. He handed the blunt to Dirty, who took three-man size hits and hacked up a lung upon exhaling. When he finished, he started swiveling his hips and dancing to the music, laughing. "Oh, hell yeah, Screw, you making this trip one worth taking, let's do it for the children!"

Dirty set up at the microphone in the booth while Screw prepared two more drinks.

With Screw back in the room, Dirty removed his notebook from his Carhartt jacket pocket. He flipped through some pages until he found some rhymes that might work. He yelled to Screw who was sipping his cup at his soundboard, looking exuberant but dazed.

"Aight, Screw! Let it rip!" yelled Dirty.

The beat kicked in, and Dirty closed his eyes and bobbed his head.

"Yo, Osiris, Yo, ODB and DJ Screw now and forever! Yo, we in this to kill, defeat."

Dirty was just riffing, trying to get into the flow. Letting the vibes wash over him. No sleep in near 48 hours and an army of chemicals coursing through his body; he was in his element. Russell Jones had vacated his body, and the parasite that was Ol' Dirty Bastard was in control. Fueled by opiates, he was free. No one could hold him down."

"I'm on THE RUN!.." Ol' Dirty Bastard delivered the line in a high-pitched rasp at a screaming volume, but crooned the last word in his manic, comedic manner.

"I'm on THE RUN!
I'm On THE RUN!
I'm FREE MOTHERFUKER!

"tired of being a lazy nigga
itchy fingas on the trigga nigga
DJ Screw with ODB, on the run
I'm free, can't stop me, sipping codeine in da warm houston sun"

Drankin the lean, forgot about mah bitch,
Smoking PCP. forgot about mah bitch
Problems gone, I'm FREE
I'm on the run, can't stop ME"

Dirty was on fire. Screw was certain they were creating something great. Something that would consecrate him as an artist. Dirty too was elated, he hadn't spit like that in months. He didn't even want to go back to New York to record for Wu Tang. He felt he was on a new cutting edge here. Hip-hop needed an avant-garde. It needed an aesthetic that antagonized its mainstream. And here it was. The most inventively bizarre rapper to ever come out of New York rapping over the chopped production of DJ Screw. This was Eric B. and Rakim. This was Ice Cube and the Bomb Squad. A meeting of minds. One mic. One deck. A legendary interplay.

To celebrate the track, the two artists sipped on lean and smoked blunts for hours. They talked. About hip-hop. Life.

Death. Drugs. Women, and their cities. They talked about what it's like to be outsiders. About what it's like to be drug addicts in a culture full of drug users who look down upon addicts. They talked about their ailing health. At some point, the personas of the two men faded with the narcotics and they were themselves again. Russell Jones and Robert Davis Jr talked until the drugs rendered them incapable of doing so anymore.

When he woke up the next morning, Screw cursed himself for over-sleeping. It was already noon, and he swore he'd get up early. Him and Dirty needed to get high, eat breakfast, and start recording again. But when he walked over to the guest room, he noticed the door was open. The bed was empty. Dirty's car was gone. He'd left. Maybe that one track was all he needed. Maybe it would carry his legacy beyond his imminent expiration date. Maybe this was ok.

CHAPTER 9

◆ crash ◆

I'm incapacitated now, slipping into the abyss. My mind. Its architecture is eroding. I'm disintegrating. Why did I make this decision to close the loop on my five-year plan? You'll never know. You'll speculate. You'll rationalize and theorize Darby Crash's suicide, but that's it. Because I'm a legend. And I'm a legend because I'm dead.

As I lie here next to the last woman to ever want what I'd never give her, everything is clear. Clearer than normal. I'm sinking deeper, I'm falling fast, but I feel joy! I've known so little, and I feel it now. With four hundred dollars' worth of dope frying my central nervous system, I'm taking back control of my own narrative. I'm erecting MYSELF as my own icon to my own cult. My flock can't abandon me now! As if I'd get old and boring and watch my legacy wither and die as I age into a homeless, dope addicted FAGGOT? Please. Not me. In death, I will be immortal. My triumph is my demise! I don't know how to change. The emptiness would have swallowed everything I created. I. Will. Not. Have. That.

Casey is getting blurrier. She said she wanted to die with me. I know she was lying. To herself, most of all. She wants to be written into my history and have my legacy. She can't have it and neither can you. It belongs to no one, and to everyone. But not to her and not to you. I'm dying now, but Paul died a long time ago. Perhaps he never lived. Maybe Paul is just the lingering confusion that never went away, I don't remember anymore. Perhaps then, she had no chance of saving him. Me. But Darby? Darby can't live without me either.

I've been considering killing myself since I was a young boy. The sad neglected boy. So banal. So ordinary. Yet, nothing ever filled that hole — the clothes, the persona, the brown and white powders — nothing sustained me. That psychotic cunt of a mother, my dead brother, nothing. The abyss. I'm in it. Closer.

They kicked me out of high school for antisocial behavior. "Mind control." Impressive, right? The scientists thought I was too "cultish." Words are power. God is dead. The great manipulator understands this. Hitler's hate. Manson's family. Bowie's cathartic, joyful deviance! He was a genius! But am I?

The great artists manipulate reality. And people. A leader creates an image that can be projected onto. In art, fascism makes sense.

I don't hate or want to kill, but denial of Hitler is denial of creative will. I'm the true fascist – the manifestation of the will of my people. My words hypnotize. I created a new world. Spengler's circle! My circle! The Germs burn! It's everything! But what is it? The great artists — the real manipulators — break that circle. I bent those around me to my own will, and my will became theirs. But... I could never change how I felt. Empty. Unloved. Pathetic.

I fucking hate art. I believe in David Bowie, Iggy Pop and Charles Manson. Here was punk rock. It needed prophets. I became one. He is called Darby Crash. And Darby Crash was a symbol. The artist who hates art and wants to destroy it. Was it real?

Heroin, speed and booze buried me inside of Darby. Paul is Darby's parasite, Darby is the host. Fuck, there were parts of Paul that I could just never bury. Darby Crash was a tornado and it sucked up everything in its path and now I'm dying and dead.

Darby needs followers. Followers need Darby. Your lives are meaningless now and henceforth.

My lyrics screamed, my flesh desecrated and defiled. As Darby I'm sanctified by violence. Paul was confused, alienated, fatherless. A sad closeted faGGot. Everything that Paul experienced as pain; his mother's contempt and abuse, his real father's absence and fake father's death, Bobby; was experienced by Darby as fuel. Pain was Darby's foundation. The burdens of Paul's soul hardened into Darby like a shield. In martyrdom, narrative becomes mythology. Darby Crash Forever! The Germs forever! Righteous excess, FOREVER!

I'm exhausted. My pain and alienation as Paul allowed me to create Darby, but Darby still carried that pain and alienation. Language, he who wields it is in control. But of himself? I don't feel in control. Language is a virus and I'm sick of hearing myself talk.

Darby Crash is just a sad little fag. The female anatomy is abject. I don't like it. Women are my mothers. The deeper that I sublimated into Darby the further I alienated the family unit. I shot up more.

My influence waned. I don't want to be a washed up faggot junkie tricking on Skid Row. I want the legend to live, so I must die. Elegant.

A family unit or a cult? Circularity. *Decline of the West.* There is no linear progression to culture, man! It all fucking loops. What is my deeper reality? The deeper reality is that Darby Crash never escaped myself. I'm back at the beginning, stuck once again with the same pain. Heroin numbs, heroin exacerbates. Who is listening? God? Do you understand?

Everything is getting dark. Thoughts are just thoughts, fleeting bits of information. For Darby (for "me"), heroin made sense. A signifier of excess. But its utilitarianism cannot be underestimated. I have been terrified of my desire since I felt it. I never had an interest in girls. I remember the first boner I got, in gym class. Humiliation: it's poison.

The terror, where did it come from? Why didn't Darby free me to be a faggot? Why couldn't my faggotry be brandished as a weapon? My entire persona was built on the image of an outsider, and I repressed the thing that made me inherently so. Paranoia, fear, anxiety, sickness of the mind.

I wasn't the only fag. There were other fags, some hard as nails. Some of those fags were way harder and more dangerous than I ever was, Maybe that's why my desire was such a hideous monster? Maybe a faggot needs to be hard. I'm soft. On the inside, I'm a scared child. Darby Crash is haunted by a scared child. And now I'm so horny that I just want to fuck but I'm scared to fuck and I'm more scared than ever and lonely and dejected.

150

I'm unfulfilled. I'm unloved because I can't love back. Donnie's sympathy wasn't love. Tony loved me, but did I love him? His boldness made me feel more shame. His lack of shame made me feel cold and alone. Sex hollows me out, and the junk can no longer suppress my desire. I'm being ripped apart by shame and horniness and sex, and death is the answer.

Asexuality was unattainable. 15 bags of junk a day I still am a loaded gun of desire. "A post-sexual superhuman?" Yeah right. More like: "Pathetic desperate unlovable faggot who hates himself so much that he became someone else." All that denial. All that shame. It met its climactic end. My death is my final signal. My last work of mass hypnosis.

The more dope I shoot the more vulnerable I am. They're predators. I can no longer control my flock. My cult turned on me. To fascinate people isn't to earn their respect (important lesson). How the fuck else would a fat, old, sad slob like Amber sink her teeth into me? It didn't matter. She could have been anyone. She could have been a fucking hippie who listened to Pink Floyd and pretended it was meaningful. The fact is, she gave me heroin. She gave me as much heroin as I wanted. The cow tried to pervert and seduce me with her disgusting body and I forgave her because I needed what she gave me and because I'm weak.

The Germs reunion. On stage, I felt the pure mystic energy of performance coursing through me once more! I felt my power channeling through the crowd and through me, a reciprocal necromancy! Darby lives!

A delusion. I'm a novelty act. At 21, I'm finished. How will I live? Turn tricks? I won't. Darby was all I had to give. I had a five year plan: become a star or die. I'm dying, baby. I said my good-byes, but there's no one left. I'll be dead, but Darby is unkillable. Suicide is glamour, rock n' roll, and magic. It makes sense.

I thought that I could break that circle, and flatten it into a straight line. I thought that I, like Bowie, would evolve. But I got caught. I looped around directly to the beginning. I couldn't excavate the truth of who I was. I was afraid of it! I was afraid of my desire. A fag. I'm plunging into the abyss, and it feels good. The fag dies with me.

I'm the bloodless version of myself. Like Bowie sang, "We had five years left to cry in (cry in)." Well, my five years are up. If you can't evolve, then die a legend. I hate poetry, but that's poetry.

Oh my god... my heart is barely beating now. Maybe one beat every five seconds.

I'm falling so fast, faster and faster. Oh my god, it feels amazing! I'm dying, but I can't die! Darby Crash will live on! I am in control, no one will take it, and I'll never lose it. I'm.... An icon. I'm remembering another song – oh man I was proud of this one. I wrote it. It was mine...

Fuck, it's so dark. It's black, I can't see. What were those lyrics? How did it go? Something like.

I'm your annihilation man
Lemme get control I've got your minds...

I can't think..... I'm..... Far.. Away.

Now I want
Your souls, le.......

....

CHAPTER 10
· therapy ·

Karl

Karl, or "Dr. Bluth" as he was fondly referred to by his patients, felt awful. The sharp spasms of pain that enveloped his chest when he moved around or sat down were getting worse. His days were numbered, this much remained clear. And what had he really achieved? He asked himself this all the time. Placing his right palm to his chest and massaging the tissue that lined his ailing heart, he realized that he didn't really know. And maybe that was OK.

He sat back at his desk and tilted his head, peaking through the blinds of his window that revealed a glimpse of Campden Street. He took a glance around his well-lit office — a couch for his patients sat in the middle of the room opposite his desk, all three walls were lined in bookshelves and his desk littered with objects presented to him as gifts from his gifted patients — he thought of those men.. Bluth was here for them, the poets of his era. He would die here to give relief to these poets who opened their souls up to the universe and left themselves vulnerable to its treacheries. They would need him. But mostly, he stayed here for Anna.

Karl had a wife. He had a successful practice with countless patients who relied on him. But, he considered while staring into space, his life was a void. Despite its fullness, it was little more than a bottomless abyss that only Anna could fill. Karl knew that his relationship with Anna was his only passion. It was an obsession that animated his all but lifeless body. He had violated every ethical principle that he had ever pledged to uphold in the decade since he met Anna at St. Stephen's Landing, and whatever misgivings he held about his conduct were pacified by the fact that he knew he'd do it all over again without the slightest apprehension. His love for Anna and his need to keep her stable and functioning was beyond a romantic love. In that absence of sexual contact — the lingering of libido left unfulfilled — something infinitely more intense than love or sex or marriage took form. He'd kill 1000 children to save Anna if he had to. He'd kill his wife. He'd die happily to prevent anything befalling his beloved Anna. If there was any reason at all that he survived the Nazis, it was so that he would one day meet and care for Anna. His perfect artist.

Karl got up from his desk and exited his office breathing in deep to prepare himself for the scolding eyes of his long-suffering and neglected wife. Walking into the bedroom to collect his medical kit and other belongings, he saw her lying on the bed and reading a book. Just looking at Theo sent chills down his spine. The degree to which he felt nothing for her — not anger, not contempt, and certainly not love — was at this point a small terror. Theo clung to her envy of Karl and Anna's relationship for as long as she could, but it had finally broken.

"Are you headed out dear?" asked Theo, dressed in a nightgown that accentuated the still rather slender and youthful figure she possessed, although the sinews of her body didn't even register to Karl.

"Yes, I have to visit a patient, but I won't be gone long."

Karl grabbed his medical kit from his nightstand, and it carried 100 tabs of heroin, 40 tabs of morphine, 50 tabs of amphetamine, and several syringes. The bag would be empty once he left Anna's.

Theo grabbed Karl's arm from where she laid, startling him, and looked directly in his eyes with a look so dismissive that it once would have castrated his very spirit.

"Why do you do that?"

"Do what?" Karl asked.

"Every day you're telling me you're going to visit 'a patient,' as if I don't know that that patient is Anna, and as if it isn't strange that you're visiting this 'patient' daily."

Bluth looked at her, and paused. He was well aware that this tick was probably annoying, given the mutual understanding that he and Theo had already developed in their marriage. Why sweeten it? It was even more patronizing for him to pretend that he had any interest in protecting Theo's feelings from his mad passion.

"I have to visit Anna," he said, looking at himself in the mirror. Karl was mildly revolted by his hairless head that looked like a bulbous mass of flesh without shape or line, and his round face that despite its thinness lacked even the slightest hint of cheekbone or any qualities that might make him conventionally attractive. Catching the reflection of Theo in the bottom right corner of that mirror, he knew that she shared that disgust. Karl's only way into the hearts of women was through his intelligence and the ability he had to project an aura of fascination. That fascination once held by Theo was now replaced by her certainty in his pathetic nature. Theo viewed him as a sexless, charmless, doddering professor who had replaced real intimacy with a bizarre and macabre psychosexual obsession with his almost asexual, heroin addicted patient. But Anna saw something mesmerizing in him, and he held onto that. The ever looming possibility of their connection burned in him like a nuclear reactor. Bluth grabbed his kit and his overcoat, coldly and dispassionately kissed his wife on the cheek, and rushed out the door. He noticed that his cock was semi-erect and formed a bulge in his wool trousers; he lived for these moments of anticipation.

Anna

It had been seven hours since she had last injected herself with heroin, and the sickness was already in the post. As she sat at her typewriter, the words ceased to emanate from her fingers. She was shivering, and noticed sweat leaking from her temples and behind her neck. She had more heroin and morphine in the house than would be necessary to ease the pain of a grievously wounded army, but dared not use any of her own. The longer she waited, the more beautiful his shot would be. It was always worth waiting for his shot.

Instead, Anna decided to kill time with amphetamines. At best, she'd get some words written down. At worst, she could clean the house. She loaded her bazooka up with 40 MG of pharmaceutical grade speed (unquestionably a high dose) and watched herself inject the spike into a vein in her vanity mirror that sat across the room against her book shelves stacked to the ceiling. The speed entering her bloodstream was like electricity across a current. Instantaneously, her heart rate elevated and her eyes became little entry points into a black abyss. She got up from the chair and started thumbing through her many books across the shelves. The books were in no particular order. Not alphabetical. Not chronological. She'd often read 10 pages of a book and then stacked it on the shelves, a testament to the turmoil of her psychological profile. She no longer read for pleasure, but for ideas. In each book she acquired a fragment from which she could collage onto her creative landscape. With few friends left, a dead son, and a dead mother who never loved her, Anna was a demon with a thirst for annihilation.

Basking in the mild paranoia of the speed enhanced delusion, Anna started rifling through her books across the shelves. Eyes watering, she was more aware that the black sun of depression that always lingered beyond the expanses of her psyche was a bit more visible beyond the horizon at the moment. She tried not to look, diverting all of her attention to her books. Jean Rhys' *Voyage in the Dark*. Sartre's *Being and Nothingness*. Friedrich Schlegel's *Lucinde*. She then picked up the recently released novel by the French pervert Alain-Robbe Grillet, *The Erasers*, and was perturbed by the fact that the novel showed real promise. At first she thought the writer nothing more than a pale imitation of her work, but he was onto something. This made Anna feel small and ordinary. Profusely sweating now, she grabbed her handkerchief from the pocket of her dress and wiped down her face. She found a copy of Kafka's *The Castle* and opened it to her favorite page.

We had more hope then than we do now, but even then our hope was
not great, only our misery, and so it has remained.

There was a time when this passage filled Anna with melancholy. Perhaps that was before she had totally succumbed to the frozen existence of junk. Perhaps that was before she was raped, when she still thought she could love. Perhaps that was before Karl. But now there was only Karl. There was only the relief that he gave her, and the tranquility that he injected into her veins. Karl was all that was beautiful.

Anna walked back to her desk and her typewriter and looked out on Notting Hill. Outside, there were men and women walking. Some of them held hands. Some of them smiled, while others wore an expression of muted existential dread. With few friends left (besides beautiful Karl, and a couple of poofs she kept on retainer), Anna was essentially a shut-in. If she wasn't able to write or paint, she would no doubt be forced to endure the faux-sympathy of those out in the world: "Poor strange woman, with her psychosis and her drugs, locked away." But she liked being locked away, in a prison of her own mind. With the drugs she could exist here forever, but at least writing gave her peculiarities some intellectual justification. The city, though it was right before her, was little more than an abstraction to her. She looked upon it like an Ensor painting. The people walking by had skulls and other demonic visages where their human faces should be. It terrified her, but it was a terror of fascination. Though she kept her distance, she never failed to derive inspiration from it while looking down on it from above. In here, with her typewriter and her dope, she let the images wash all over her. With the amphetamine still buzzing inside her brain but obscuring the condition of her dope sickness less and less by the second, she averted her eyes back to her typewriter. She was getting impatient for the good part of her day.

Anna was working on a book, in addition to a few essays that she planned on having published by the journal. Since becoming Anna Kavan and ditching both the name that she was born with (Helen) and the name that was forced on her by that brutal pig, her word had grown increasingly preoccupied with her mad interiority. She believed that the surrealists were frauds; with his male, middle-class fetishization of psychosis, Anna thought that Bréton only flirted with and exploited that which she had no choice but to live inside. She began typing away, but the speed failed to give her any of the clarity that the drug is known for. She could only type words. "Sick," "flummoxed," "despair," "cold," "slipping," "darkness," "confused," and "alone."

Anna understood her writing to be utterly self-absorbed, and was perfectly secure in this knowledge. Her singularly detached existence coupled with her extreme instability, she knew, gave her a perspective that at least some readers would be compelled by. Her last novel, *A Scarcity of Love*, fictionalized her experience of the cunt passing away and writing her out of the will. It was, perhaps, a bit too grounded in the material world. Rage is so banal, she now realized. This novel, which she planned on calling *Eagle's Nest*, would also be based in reality, but in the reality of the world she lived in. A reality of interiority, disconnected from everything outside. The window that separated Anna between her office and the city was the metaphysical walls between dimensions. Anna was plagued by a troubling thought that her life wasn't actually happening. She was always one step removed from catatonia, and only Karl and heroin held her back from slipping into it. This was the state that she was finally trying to render to language. So far, it was proving more difficult than she had hoped.

"When is he going to be here?" she thought.

Twiddling her thumbs and massaging the back of her neck, the evacuation of dope from Anna's receptors was slowly forcing her to confront the thoughts that she typically did her damnedest to suppress. While genuine and ferocious – her madness and melancholy, she understood as weapons. She used them to manipulate people. To manipulate Karl, especially. The difference between Karl and the other men that had loved her was that Karl wanted nothing of her. He only wanted her to write. With all the ethical boundaries that he had crossed, sex was one that he couldn't bring himself to be on the other side of. Thus, their relationship was in a permanent limbo of mutual fascination, need, and dependence. Sex was a spectral presence in their partnership. Of course, sex had never been of much interest to Anna, not since she was very young. She didn't hate it exactly – but unlike heroin, sex was a pleasure that brought her closer to the chaos of her condition. While heroin suspended her in a frozen ambience of controlled anxiety — she often thought of the drug as the hand of a strong, kind man who was grasping hers as she hung over the edge of a mountain, a vast abyss of certain death below — sex was the catalyst for the demons to overtake her. She had had good experiences with sex, but no memories of sex burned brighter than the violence she endured at the hands of Donald, or those of Stuart's castrated disappointment when he too realized that she no longer wanted or craved him. Her relationship with Karl, however sexless, was the most intense connection with a man she had ever felt. The absence of sex only accentuated the eroticism of their interactions. While she hated his

162

wife as any normal "other woman" would, she didn't want Karl to leave her. His lack of availability coupled with his total devotion to her was like those moments before orgasm lingered on forever, collapsed in a temporal frame that only they could inhabit. Having consumed nothing but cigarettes, heroin and speed all day, Anna felt a tightness in her stomach and bile suddenly gnawed at her chest.

She sprinted out of her office down the ornate, Victorian halls lined with her paintings, into the bathroom and barely made it to the toilet before she was gargling vomit from her mouth. With puke half in the bowl and half on the floor, she collapsed her back against the edge of the toilet to gather herself. After a few moments of heavy breathing, she got up and looked at her reflection in the mirror lined in a golden frame. Her pupils were black opals, and her color was pallid. Nevertheless, with Karl her vulnerability was the point. It's what he craved, she knew this. After she washed the puke from the floor, her face, and her hands, she applied pink lipstick and puckered her lips. There was a knock at the door.

He's here!

Anna and Karl

With an exuberant smile across her face, Anna rushed to the door. Her heart pulsated with an authenticity that the stimulation of amphetamines couldn't possibly be responsible for. Karl was flushed. A decade of near daily visits, and still his visits with Anna made him nervous and giddy. When she opened the door, the smile she wore across her pale, skinny face eradicated his defenses. Her thin and drawn-on eyebrows, her bleach blonde bob, her fashionably understated clothes, her eyes full of joy, need, and craving; she was everything.

Without speaking, Bluth took Anna's hands into his own and held them down at her hips. He kissed her on both cheeks, holding his lips in place for just a pause longer than is typically cordial. Anna breathed in deep, her body racked with sweat and chills as the amphetamine wore off and the opiate cravings became impossible to ignore, and basked in his embrace.

"Hello, Karl."

"How are you?"

"I'm well, but come in. We can talk more."

As one walked into Anna's house, there was a den to the right of the foyer. As they had done hundreds of times before, they walked into it hand in hand and took their respective seats separated by a coffee table empty save for a model globe that was saturated in earth tones and spun from a wooden handle.

Sitting down, Anna watched Karl as he emptied his medical kit, smirking about the quantity of substances that he loaded onto the table (he brought almost the same amount of drugs with him only yesterday, knowing fully well that Anna couldn't possibly have used all of it already).

"How many times have you used today?" asked Karl. Anna, whose eyes were watering and was fighting against the yawns of withdrawal, looked up at Karl listlessly. "Just once, but I also used some amphetamine to try and get some writing done."

The beauty in their love announced itself in what was unsaid. In the silences, in the manipulations that were ever present but tacitly condoned, and in all the possibilities that would never be realized, was a connection that could never be known to those outside of it.

"You look a little under the weather," said Karl. "Let's fix you up."

Karl prepared a shot of 40 MG of Dia-Morphine, sucking the viscous substance back into the bazooka. Anna did her part in tying a rubber tourniquet around her thigh to find a vein, as she was having increasing trouble finding usable veins in her arms. They were beginning to collapse.

Karl walked past the globe and Anna leaned back into her chair, opening her legs up slowly to reveal the vein pulsating just to the left of her crotch. When Karl approached the injection site with the bazooka, she removed her hand from the vein to reveal a hairless patch of flesh. She squeezed Karl's shoulder with her hand. Time was frozen in the room, like they were the only two living beings in a dimension made of the energies of their imaginations.

The spike penetrated Anna's skin and she let out a small gasp in response. Karl pulled back the bazooka and a small flood of red fluid gushed from the tiny flesh opening back into it. Staring directly into Anna's eyes and biting the lower corner of his lip, Karl nodded at her. She let go of the band, and it flopped back onto the floor. Karl, without breaking eye contact, pushed it back into her one more time, and Anna slightly purred and moaned

165

with the fluid now burning inside of her. The relief it gave her was instantaneous, and Anna basked in the clarity of her new sickness free body. Karl, in a limbo of both desire and perverse fascination, watched in awe as Anna's head fell backwards and the eyes rolled into the back of her forehead. After a few moments, she smiled, which gratified Karl and made him feel like a man.

Karl allowed Anna to enjoy the satisfaction of the drug before they talked. He was well aware that there was very little that was clinically therapeutic about their interactions anymore, and to the degree that he was helping her it was only his willingness to bypass those clinical regulations that facilitated her care. They were friends, and they were almost lovers, but used the doctor-patient relationship to justify the bizarreness of their prolonged engagement. Karl never believed much in therapy anyways. He hated therapy. He despised doctors. He wanted to be an artist, he wanted to write, but Hitler denied him that desire. So he escaped Germany and he became a psychiatrist. He came to despise Krapelin and the reductive ways that his theories diagnosed psychosis. Bluth, a romantic at heart, viewed madness as essential to the creative process. He had treated many artists, but none more so than Anna. Anna was always on the verge, and he convinced himself that the drugs kept her making art. She was, in a way, his work of art. His vessel. And however manipulative this might sound, she was manipulating him equally. Karl was facilitating her slow death, but he hoped that his love, friendship, and opiates could allow the writer to evade pathologizing her melancholy and instead take her pain and funnel it into crackling, creative energy. Her sadness was mesmerizing.

"So, how's Theo?" Anna asked, coyly.

"She's fine," he quickly changed the subject. "How are you?"

Anna loved how their exchanges always began in stark banality. Karl, to this very day, was always trying to convince himself that there was anything normal about their life together. She loved that he all but spiritually left his wife and dedicated all his energy to her, and yet they never even made love. And he still very much lived with his wife.

"Writing has been hard today," she admitted. "I don't know why exactly. Perhaps it's that I've never attempted to render my emotional state of being to words so directly. I don't think anyone could understand how I actually think or feel. It's like I'm a mutant. You're the only one who has ever got it, really."

A jolt of feeling blasted through Karl's body. "Maybe we're both mutants," he said, chuckling. "Or aliens. But surely this isn't the first time you've given your characters life through unconscious tension."

Anna paused to consider this clever comment by her best critic. "You're right, what's different is that there seems to be no events in this book other than those that happen internally. But that is, I suppose, how I live. I feel neither dead nor alive. I feel alive now, but not usually."

Karl and Anna lived in constant fear over the other's death. Karl was sometimes paralyzed by the idea that his drugs would be used by Anna to kill herself accidentally or deliberately, and Anna worried that Karl's heart condition would take him away from her prematurely.

167

"Have you been thinking about death again?" asked Karl.

"You know very well that I'm always thinking about death," she responded, staring at Karl with a gesture that made her look as if frozen within an iceberg. "I don't think I've ever been alive. Not since I was a girl, really. Not since I was abandoned. Sometimes I think my art is more valid because it's like the document of a living dead girl."

Karl was dumbfounded by the profundity of her statement. She said something this beautiful and painful at least once a day.

Anna felt much calmer than she had earlier. She wanted to use more drugs, but still felt it was necessary to shield the doctor from the extremity of her use (even though he fully knew the extent of her addiction).

"Do you want me to make any tea or anything?" she asked.

"No, I'm fine. I can't stay much longer."

Anna internalized Karl's briefer visits as nothing short of a small but devastating breakup. She cracked her neck and then looked right back at him, hoping she could start a dialog that would get him to stay longer.

"Do you ever worry that you're just my enabler?" asked Anna, shocked at the pointedness of her own question and regretting that she had even said it.

Karl found himself flustered. He indeed did hold that concern. Constantly. But why would she ask him now?

"Well, I worry about a lot of things," said Karl. "I worry that I've projected my own idealism onto you, which has given you something of an intellectual justification for your addiction."

Anna nodded, and for the first time in years, she felt the faintest whisper of sexual arousal.

"I worry that I lie to myself, and to you, and to my wife, and to everyone about what this is between you and I. I worry that our friendship isn't a friendship at all, but a perversion. A fetish."

"How am I your fetish?" asked Anna.

"I.... I'm not sure. I think I've just always believed in drugs as a mechanism for the artist to channel his madness. So I've convinced myself that by facilitating your writing with drugs, by keeping your madness cohesive and preventing it from subsuming your psyche - I've facilitated your art."

Anna was moistened, and flooded with desire. She sat at the edge of her seat, wondering what would happen if she approached him. "Go on," she said.

"I feel like your work is both of ours, Anna. It's like it belongs to both of us, and this thing that we do is part of our sick, perverted process."

"Because it is," she responded.

Karl was amazed by what she just said, and found himself firmly erect as Anna got up from her seat, walked past the globe, and climbed onto his lap. Neither of them had yearned for erotic contact like this in decades, or maybe ever. Anna locked her small, pouty lips onto the wide mouth of Karl and slid her tongue into his mouth. She wriggled on top of him, and his cock kept getting harder. She momentarily got up, hacked her skirt up, and took her panties off. She took Karl's massive, hairy hand and jammed his pointed finger into her cunt. Karl found himself amazed at how wet it was, given Anna's age and the extent of her opioid use. With his fingers inside her, Anna undid his pants and took his cock out. She was shocked by the size of it. Its length was around 9 inches, and its width was about that of a coin. She gestured herself atop him once more, and slid the tip of his cock up and down her cunt to lather it up.

Karl, blinded with desire, felt a sharp pain in his chest. He ignored it for a moment, and then it barreled him over. "Aghhhhhhh!" he shrieked, and threw Anna to the floor as he fell face forward. Karl cracked his head on the globe table, and passed out.

Several minutes later, Karl awoke to Anna on the phone with the hospital, shrieking with fear. After a few moments, he said, "Stop, I'm fine."

She rushed over to him, "I thought you were going to die, my god, are you OK?" Karl assured her that he was, and asked that she get him some water. When she came back with the glass, he apologized about his physical condition.

"You have absolutely nothing to apologize for," she said, "It's my fault."

Karl stroked her smooth skin, and assured her that nothing between them would change. And he meant it.

"I best head home," said Karl. "Would you like me to prepare you another shot before I leave?"

"That would be lovely, thank you."

Karl loaded the bazooka once more, and spiked Anna up much the same way that he had earlier and many times before. This was to be their intimacy. This was their connection. It didn't make what they had any less real.

Karl

When Karl got back to his flat, Theo was already asleep, and he felt a wave of relief over that matter. Without trying to, his mind inevitably turned to what had just transpired at Anna's house. He felt over-extended, but also full of need. He tried to masturbate in his office, but this only made him feel ridiculous. If he couldn't have Anna the way most men have their women, he decided, then he wanted to feel what she felt. He wanted to experience the world as she did to some small extent. He went to his medicine cabinet and grabbed some Dia-Morphine. He loaded the bazooka with the junk, wrapped the tourniquet around his arm, and put the needle into a bulbous vein in his right forearm. He hoped to see Anna in his dreams.

CHAPTER 11

✦ at annina nosei ✦

Fuck you dad. Fuck you and your three-piece suit, your contempt and your rage and your inability to control yourself and to love anyone outside yourself. Fuck you mom. You crazy fucking cunt. My hatred for you has erased any love that was once there. I don't feel it. Fuck you to the cannibals and the fame whores and the needy junkies and the faggot artists who want to steal what is rightfully mine. You can't have what is mine, I'll spend it on Comme des Garçons and shoot it up my arms with a diamond needle before I let any of you have a fucking thing. I'm the man with the golden arm and a platinum cock. Anonymity? You thought I wanted to be pure? HAH! I'm here to get rich and be worshipped. Put me in history. Good or evil, irrelevant. I'll be in it. You won't. Rich bourgeois college educated bogus philosophy reading cock sucking liberals. Coming here into this basement, with your questions. I have no answers, you tasteless old twat! Your money though, it smells delicious. Yeah, I'll have some of that. I'd rather you just call me a nigger than be your monkey. I'll be a coon colored in green, only as black as you need me to be. I'm going to be a star, shining brighter than Hendrix soloing the national anthem and channeling all the energies of the transcendent orgasm, shooting nut and disconnecting from what is here. Junk always brings me down, so why not? I can float up, soaring higher than you'll ever go, and then inject that brown and comfortably inhabit my body once more. That, motherfucker, is freedom! Mail me the check, take the painting and go, fraudulent scum. Everyone I've

ever known or ever loved could die right now and I'd feel nothing. No. No....
I would feel something. I'd feel happy. Yes! I'd be ecstatic that you were dead
because then I'd be alone to enjoy what I earned my fucking self. I'd sit on a
throne in peace and quiet and I'd listen to Miles and bliss out on the sheer ecstasy
of the death of the world around me. Oh, man....What a beautiful thought.

Constipated and lost in the poetic patterns of his daydreams, Jean-Michel was feeling particularly morose today. Sitting on the toilet, he tried with every ounce of his strength to push a shit out of his asshole. Days had gone by since he had last taken one, and he knew that wasn't healthy. Living on candy, heroin, and cocaine, he couldn't remember the last time he ate something resembling a normal meal. Weeks? Months, even? His typical strategy was to start the morning with two lines of cocaine he hoped would stimulate his bowels against the opioid-induced constipation. He'd make sure to not use heroin for the first hours he was awake, solely to try and pass a bowel movement. It seldom worked. As of late, he'd rupture his asshole all for some skinny rings of shit (that took rolls of toilet paper to wipe despite barely registering in the toilet) and blood to seep into the toilet water. Unsatisfying, no doubt. Jean-Michel, getting exhausted in his efforts, exerted one more heroic push.

"Hmmmmmmmmmmmmerrrrrrrrrrrrrrrrr...."

Nothing. He took a piece of toilet paper, folded it, and wetted it under the faucet. He wiped the shit smelling sweat from his ass. Washing his hands, he saw the sweat droplets forming around his eyes and on his neck and felt the chills and shivers down his spine. No bother, he'd been up for a couple hours. He could now fix and get to work.

Jean-Michel had used heroin for years but didn't tell anyone about it. Unlike marijuana and cocaine whose use he had turned into a spectacle…walking towards the windows that overlooked Crosby St., he pondered what it was about heroin that he felt needed hiding these last few years? Opening his blinds one by one, he let three glorious blasts of sunlight rush into the room and illuminate a wide open space, littered in paint, materials, canvases, drug paraphernalia, pizza boxes, and a coffee table filled with syringes, rolled up dollar bills, roaches, style magazines, and cassette tapes. He considered himself "a brand," the image that he'd deliberately cultivated on his path towards success. "Jean-Michel Basquiat, The Radiant Child," as that insufferable queer Rene referred to him as in the Artforum article. Yet he thought, Rene did have a point, despite how annoying and needy he could be. Jean-Michel wanted to *radiate*. He wanted to be special – to glow, to be seen as something exotic and full of life. He felt enraged whenever he thought about how the artworld treated him like this primitive artifact. "Hah," he chuckled to himself, looking out onto the streets – his kingdom. Jean-Michel resented everyone who had ever helped him. He outright hated those who loved him. They were means to his ends: fame, the status of a legend. Pot and coke were accessories to the Radiant Child brand: jazz music, street poetry, dancing, the Mudd Club, sex (so much sex).

But heroin? Heroin was such a cliché. It was passé. Being a junkie? That's so boring – so utterly banal! Would people think of him as just another rich, dope shooting artist who would burn out and fade away? Or, has the myth already taken on a life of its own? Maybe it was out of his hands now, maybe he already secured his position in the zeitgeist…

It didn't matter. The cat was out of the bag. Since he'd gotten back from Paris, his junk use had escalated, and people were talking about it. "Whatever," thought Jean-Michel, who had picked a roach up off of the coffee table, lit it and inhaled the little cannabis left. He coughed abruptly, spitting a loogie into the pizza box tucked beneath the table. Jean-Michel had to keep moving. He would sometimes awake from a slumber, panicked over the singular fear of failure. He worried that if he stopped for one moment, then people would see through the Radiant Child and into the soul of Jean-Michel: a weak, effeminate, middle class boy who was afraid of his father and hated his mother. "There's nothing fuckin special about that," he thought, emptying the remnants of a bag of cocaine onto his hand and sniffing fiercely. There was blood in his nostrils, and he worried that he had deviated his septum. Fuck it.

He reached into his silk bathrobe's pocket to grab his works. He'd bought roughly seven grams of heroin from Jeffrey Bretschneider, who lived on 23rd St. Jean-Michel thought it was curious that his dealer was holding such large quantities of dope all of a sudden. Jeffrey had been his coke man for a while, and he'd spend days on end there blasting off and chatting – dancing with the pretty coke whores. But it seemed like as soon as folks on the scene learned of Jean-Michel's taste for the brown, that Jeffrey had the brown. Jean-Michel put it out of his mind, it was too early for that kind of paranoia. Jean-Michel sprinkled some junk over a crack rock, curious about whether it would be possible to "turbo charge the dragon." Just as he lit the crack pipe, he heard his name called from the bedroom.

"Jean-Miicheell, are you still here in the apartment?"

He had totally forgotten that bitch was still here.

Jean-Michel, muttering under his breath, "Yeah, I'm here."

"What did you say Jean?" she yelled back, barely distinguishable through her Ukrainian accent.

Annoyed and distressed, he huffed before yelling, "I'm in the fucking living room!"

She walked out of his bedroom like it was 8am, when it was already 1 pm. Completely naked, she walked up to him on the couch in front of the coffee table. She climbed into his lap, facing forward, and pressed her tits into his face. She was stunning in a totally boring model sort of way, sharp cheekbones and voluptuous blond hair. A curved mouth she accentuated by biting on her lower lip as an affective gesture. Her Chanel No. 5 from last night was fading, which gave her sensuousness a spectral quality. Whatever her charms, this bitch had no more need to be here. As far as he was concerned, her allure had worn off. Jean-Michel had a day planned and she wasn't to be a part of it. He pushed her off of him, trying to seem playful but hoping she would get the hint.

"I'm so escited fo' your opening tonight Jean," she said. "To see how dey adore you. To meet your friends."

Jean-Michel didn't even know her name and had no clue what sweet nothings he had filled her head with last night. He didn't even remember fucking her, though something was telling him he did. This thought made him worry for a moment; he had been spreading gonorrhea again. When he realized he was about to never see this woman though, he came to his senses.

"Well, what do you want to do today, Jean? We can get lunch before yo big night!"

Losing patience, Jean-Michel replied, "Look, what do you think this is?"

Her face looked confused, the cute biting of her lower lip morphed into a nervous sucking sensation. It was bound to leave a mark. "What?" she said.

"I don't know you, I don't remember how we got here and I sure as fuck don't know why you're still here or why you think I'm bringing you tonight to my first fucking solo show." Jean-Michel's voice never elevated, allowing him to mask cruelty under an almost poetic tone. "So, I'm going to need you to get on out of here."

The poor girl's makeup was running off in tears. She was horrified. Holding back sobs, she gathered her things and vacated the Crosby St. loft. To celebrate the silence, Jean-Michel thumbed through his cassettes and decided on a copy of *Bird and Diz*, the 1952 collaboration between Charlie Parker and Dizzy Gillespie. He closed his eyes and leaned his head back while "My Melancholy Baby" was playing. Charlie's horn solo was like the unpredictable energies of Santeria conjured forth as auditory power. He was finally able to chase the turbo charged dragon. The crack immediately spiked his heart rate before exhalation, and after exhalation..... "Damnn..." The euphoric intensity was profound, and the sensation of a tribal drum in his ears, "dum dum dum dum.....," gave Charlie and Dizzy a synthetic industrial twinge. The heroin, however, had little effect. The turbo charged dragon was a failure. Jean-Michel grabbed a used syringe (only a couple times used, however), and cooked a shot. He injected three bags into the pulsating vein of his right arm.

Jean-Michel never stopped; his energy was immense even in the speedball. He immediately started jotting down notes in his little pads. Writing words and sentences that came to his mind.

Nicotine walks on eggshells medicated....
A "youth" with "crow syndrome"
"Arab singing"

Jean-Michel rolled a joint with one part cannabis and one part tobacco, getting pieces of both substances stuck in his teeth as he licked the spliff tight. He sucked it down quick, within six puffs, and found himself deliriously narcotized. His paranoia was running wild, and for a moment he was sure the CIA wanted to kill him because he was a rich and famous black man. No, that can't be true, he thought. His delusions sometimes amused him — he simultaneously knew they were delusions and, yet, the physical sensations of extreme anxiety they produced lingered. How can one know something is a fantasy while still, physically, believing it is real? "Now that's fucking far out," Jean-Michel muttered out loud, to no one in particular. Pacing back and forth, he decided to change the tapes. He put on Hendrix's *Band of Gypsies*. Jimi's opening riffs on "Who Knows" sent Jean-Michel swaying from side to side...

They all are after me. The CIA, the FBI, all of them want me dead because they can't let my vibes lead the world to truth and beauty.... Hah! They are too dumb to know that they should kill me! They think I'm a slave locked in that fuckin' basement, painting away! They are my slaves! Enslaved to my vibes! I conjure devil worship magic because I can channel what's beyond, all that beauty that no one else can see, I fuckin' see it! Am I being exploited? Hah! Annina would fucking kill herself if I decided to burn everything I made. That's pure power, baby! SHE THINKS I'M A CIRCUS ACT! I'm the grifter at the circus! I'm hustling that bitch! I'm hustling all of these bitches. Their admiration means something to me only insomuch as it validates what I already know: I am Van Gogh, I am fucking Jesus! If you find me, you'll find divine truth! God damn, god damn...

The phone rang and snapped Jean-Michel out of his daydream. He stopped dancing to walk over to answer it.

"Yeah?" he answered.

"Hey, Jean, it's me," it was Jean-Michel's studio assistant. "Sorry that I'm running late, last night was wild! I can't breathe through my nose! Are you alright? How are you feeling?"

Jean-Michel wasn't quite sure what his assistant was referring to exactly; assumedly they were partying hard last night? He could hardly remember the specifics of his nights anymore: all time was bleeding together as one cohesive unit the further he plunged into addiction and narcissistic madness. "Yeah, I'm fine, can you get the fuck over here? We have to sign these paintings and you're better at it than I am!"

"What's that Jean? I can't hear it over the music!"

Jean-Michel, flustered and stoned, yelled, "JUST GET THE FUCK OVER HERE!"

"Yeah, yeah, all right Jean. I'm coming."

Jean-Michel slammed the phone, its smash barely audible over the barrage of Hendrix's "Machine Gun" riffs. He waltzed back over to the couch in a kind of two-step dance-walk. His black and white pinstripe bathrobe was open, exposing his chest and his large penis flopping as he moved. He prepared another shot and injected it into the vein in his left wrist. It pinched and bled, which he cleaned by bringing his wrist to his mouth. He briefly smoked a joint and nodded out before slapping his face back into reality, deciding to get dressed.

Jean-Michel picked through his disorganized closet. There were as many clothes on the floor as there were hanging in it (when Suzanne lived here, he was able to manipulate her into doing all the household work). Knowing he wouldn't want to change again before the opening tonight, Jean-Michel tried to find a suitable outfit that would carry him through the night. An atonal static blared from the subwoofers as the Hendrix tape skipped, having ended some minutes ago. He first tried on a grey wool Ralph Lauren sweater with a paint-splattered pair of black jeans that he'd wear with motorcycle boots. No, too angsty. Too no wave. This was to be his night of glory. Jean-Michel flipped through his suits. There was a Commes des Garçons suit with unfinished hem at sleeves and ankles, giving an alluring deconstructed and ratty feel. No. It'd have to be Armani. Jean-Michel looked at his suit and saw his own contradictions within it. It was a work of divine craftsmanship that Jean-Michel fetishized but also had little emotional attachment to. It was covered in paint, signaling his devil-may-care attitude. But it wasn't really an apathetic, cool stance. It was deliberate. Everything in his life was deliberate and spoke to the polarities he embodied. He grew up lonely, typical of a middle class kid. His father was distant and brutal; he only knew how to parent with emotional abuse and, occasionally, with his fists. But Jean-Michel didn't grow up on the mean streets, and the stereotypical black urban struggle is one that he had no connection to. His pain was very common and boring for an artist, a middle class alienation. Jean-Michel, his thoughts spiraling out of control as he inhaled another hit of the rock cocaine, wondered if those months he spent living in Washington Square Park panhandling were his sincere attempt to exorcise that background, or if it was mere performance. He must have known on some level that it would make good fodder for his artistic resume. When he started making money, he wanted to spend it on everything: drugs, suits, apartments, limos, food. Everything. But he could never divorce himself from an old middle class temperance, a repulsion towards vulgar displays of wealth. So, paint on his suits, money falling out of his pockets, inability to open bank accounts, all of these served to make people think that he didn't care about money. Even though he did, even when he didn't. Jean-Michel was hardly 22 years old and he was exhausted by himself.

The suit looked, well, impeccable, Jean-Michel thought. The drugs had not yet softened the athletic sinews of his body that he'd hardened as a high school track athlete. Looking in the mirror, he contorted his frame, in awe of his own youthful agility. He stepped back a foot and stretched downward to touch his toes, breathing in and out to feel the tensions vacate his body. When he rose back upwards, he exhaled one final time, reaching his hands above his head. He felt transcendent. Godly.

Tonight is the motherfucking night, every night is the fucking night. I might not be long for this world but god fucking damn it I will rule while I am here. I am Commodus, I'm Haile Selassie. A king, the emperor. I can't be overthrown because my divine will is God-given, baby! Its energy flows throughout my body and out my fingertips. I see the future, it looks bleak. But it's beautiful. Fire, death and destruction. I can't wait. I. Can't. Wait.

The buzzer went off. Stephen had finally made it to work. Jean-Michel snapped out of his stupor. His heart rate was jacked through the roof, and he sizzled with paranoia and nervous energy. "Too much crack," he thought to himself. At a certain amount of crack intake, not even a shot of heroin can soothe the edge. He got up from the couch to buzz his assistant Stephen in.

Stephen was a small, slender black man with a 1960s James Brown bouffant afro. When standing next to Jean-Michel — who stood at an elegant, elongated 6 ft and with an athletic shoulder build — he seemed made for the role of "Jean-Michel sidekick." He wore New Wave-leaning tweed suits in the exact same style that Jean-Michel did. He was smaller, cloaked in an aura of subservience, docility and eagerness that made other people weary of him. And it was clear to anyone that Stephen was worshipful of Jean-Michel and would do anything for him AND to be just like him. This was what Jean-Michel wanted: a patsy. A lackey. Jean-Michel grinned while looking at his servant. The more famous and richer he got, the more he enjoyed the power he had over other human beings. Stephen was useful to him at the moment, but Jean-Michel relished for the day when he could discard this young man. He was going to enjoy Stephen's pain very, very much.

"Where the fuck you been, man?" Jean-Michel asked.

"I'm sorry Jean, I was hungover as fuck this morning. I tried to snap myself out of it but…"

"Enough man, whatever. It's fine. Let's put the finishing touches on these paintings so we can get them over to Annina's, we're running out of time." Jean-Michel didn't quite care whether these paintings made it to the show in time, as his contempt for his dealer Annina Nosei was reaching its apex. He really despised her. He couldn't stand the rumors about him being a slave these last couple years, locked in Annina's basement coked out of his mind, occasionally chibbing on his heroin habit in private, painting in overdrive (though it was basically an open secret that he was using seriously hard drugs in that basement, Annina knew all about his activities, she simply didn't care so long as he was painting, she's an evil cunt of the highest order, but evil cunts can be useful in the short term when trying to make it rich). But their insistence on the term "slave" was more proof that these white artworld hanger-ons had not one fucking clue how to interact with a black man. And yet, at the same time, Jean-Michel knew that the implications were basically true. He was absolutely being exploited, but he also longed to be so, you dig? Exploitation is a precondition of fame. To be a star you have to be a whore first. He knew that Annina saw him as little more than a cash machine and a good piece of branding for her own ambitions. "The Radiant Child." The exotic black artist with his "primitive" use of symbols and language and his radical figuration which seemed to channel the ghosts of a spirit world that, in these people's minds, could only be channeled by a black man. Jean-Michel allowed himself to be exoticized because he wanted to be a famous artist, but we all resent the things that we desire, no? The desire for fame and recognition is *jouissance*. No denying that.

This cunt can manipulate and exploit this beautiful piece of black ass all she wants! It's the fucking 1980s, baby! Even magic itself gets sold. It's all the same to me. My goals are simple. Enough money to spend the rest of my life stoned. I

will get high and fuck and be admired and I will feel their jealousy and contempt
and that shit will get me hard. Why you asking me all of these fucking questions?
Why do I use these words? Why do I use these symbols? Because I fucking do!
Because I dig the vibe. Miles had those vibes when he hit those notes. Sugar
Ray had those vibes when he threw out that right hook, you know what I mean?
I will make you rich and send you on your way, just leave me the fuck alone.

"Jean, you good man?" asked Stephen.

Jean-Michel had a stupefied look across his face. A muted shit-eating grin. His eyes were crossed in the kind of way you see people look during religious fervor at a Pentecostal church. He snapped back into reality.

"Yeah, I'm good. Let's get to work."

"Sure thing man. Yo, is it alright if I get a little high though, real quick? I got the kind of headache that makes men kill, you know what I'm saying?"

"Yeah, whatever. We'll both get high."

Stephen went over to the couch and prepared himself two heaving lines of cocaine and a joint. He had tried junk once but didn't like it, which Jean-Michel begrudgingly respected. Jean-Michel grabbed his cassette of PiL's *Metal Box* from the tape rack, put it on and set it to a conversational volume, and walked back to the couch to prepare himself a shot.

"Man, the Mudd was on last night! What did you think about *The Cramps* man? I really like their vibe," said Stephen, who dropped his head to the coffee table, sucked a line through a $100 bill up his nose and aimed his face to the sky like he was looking right at god, gagging on the drip and almost regurgitating last night's alcohol.

Jean-Michel laughed at how very green his studio assistant was, "Fuckin' christ man, be careful sucking down lines like that. *The Cramps?* Yeah, they're cool. Whatever."

Stephen lit the joint as Jean-Michel was pressing the needle into his arm. Stephen was fascinated by Jean-Michel's opiated ritual; the way his eyes would flutter back when the drug hit took on an angelic quality, if you watched him in a certain light. It was like there was an invisible spotlight on him; like a lounge performance when the music goes silent, the lights go out, and then a single blast of illumination shines upon a vocalist center stage who looks up at the audience with jarring intensity before tearing the house down with a sublime solo. Jean-Michel was the whole show. As an image, Stephen thought, he was one rife with symbolic potential. Hanging with Jean-Michel often felt like living in an experimental video.

"So," said Stephen. "That was pretty intense last night with Suzanne. I can't believe she hasn't taken the hint yet man. When she saw you dancing with that girl…" Stephen handed Jean-Michel the joint, who'd been nodding from the large quantity of heroin he'd just injected. Jean-Michel stood up with righteous haste and swatted it out of his hand. Who the fuck was this nobody to ask him about his life, his relationship? Jean-Michel pointed his finger right in Stephen's face and stared into his eyes with an icy murderous glare.

"Stephen, you ever ask me about Suzanne ever again, I'm going to boot your ass on the street and ruin your life, OK? No, fuck that.

You ever ask me about anything related to who I fuck, or who I do drugs with, or what drugs I do, you're gone. No, fuck that! Just don't ask me any questions, at all, you work for me! We cool but you aren't my friend."

The joint was burning the threaded fabrics of the rug. Stephen's face was drained of enthusiasm. Jean-Michel chuckled when he realized he'd never seen a black man turn white as a ghost before.

"I'm sorry, Stephen, I'm high as a kite right now. We good, man."

"Jean, I didn't mean to…"

"It's all good, baby. Chill."

Stephen, reassured, retrieved the joint from the floor and took one more hit before emptying it into an ashtray. Jean-Michel momentarily danced to the hypnotic sleaze funk of Jah Wobble's unmistakable bass stylings, and let his head drift in the language of John Lydon…

Seeing in your eyes
Seeing in your eyes
Never really know
Never realize
Silence in your eyes
Silence in your eyes

Just as Jean-Michel was assorting his paints to make last minute additions to the final three paintings in the show, the buzzer rang once more. Jean-Michel, still shockingly functional and mobile given the heart-stopping number of substances running through his body, walked over to the intercom and asked who was there. "Who is it?"

"It's me you fucking black beauty, Jean! Buzz me up, gorgeous!"

It was Rene Ricard. Jean-Michel had little patience for the old faggot right now, but nonetheless still felt like he owed him for the Artforum article from a few months back. He considered ways in which he could tell Rene to piss off without hurting the aging queer's feelings (and thus, alienating his most prominent supportive critic).

"Hey Rene, man," said Jean-Michel. "Stephen and I are just putting finishing touches on these last few paintings for the night, but we're almost about to head out. I'll catch you at the opening though, that cool?"

"Oh fuck off you whore!" said Rene, "Let me up, bitch! I want to see what you're working on!"

Jean-Michel — the itch under his nose immensely irritating, but also pleasurable in that strange dopey way — relented, sighed outwards, and buzzed the poet in.

Rene waltzed right in, and yelled "Good afternoon, faggots!" and wrapped his arms around Jean-Michel for a weird paternal hug.

"My beauty, how are you?" asked Rene.

Jean-Michel couldn't help but laugh, "I'm good Rene, thanks for stopping by."

"And how is he," Rene asked, placing his hand around Jean-Michel's cock that was outlined by the Armani trousers, "My god, girthy as ever! A real beauty, I'd say!" Rene sniffed and raised the hand that he had just grasped the artist's cock with, noticing a foul smell wafting from it. "Jesus!" said Rene. "You still haven't gotten that case of the clap treated yet? Your magnificent cock is going to fall off at this rate! Aren't you embarrassed about spreading this foulness to all your girlfriends? Have they not told each other to be weary of you and your stinky, leaky, gigantic cock yet?"

Blushing, "Well, as long as it stays big, they don't seem to mind the smell!"

With rip-roaring laughter, Rene replied, "You filthy black beauty you! That's just wonderful! I suppose you're right, the biggest cock in the room might be a filthy diseased thing, but it's still the biggest cock in the room, no doubt!"

Jean-Michel was laughing hysterically now. "I'll get it treated, soon, I swear." Rene had a quality that made it impossible to be angry at him even when he was atrociously annoying and unpleasant. Rene looked good. He was wearing a nicely pressed navy sweater with a white collared shirt beneath. The leather jacket he'd started wearing seemed a bit try-hard — Jean-Michel wondered if he was trying to mimic the fashion sense of Mapplethorpe, who was the biggest queer in New York at that point — but he, more or less, pulled it off. He was balding, but didn't hide it, which oozed confidence. Jean-Michel liked Rene because he was odd and charismatic but didn't come off like he was trying to be odd or charismatic. In a city full of desperate social climbers, that was an enviable quality.

"You look good Rene, how you doing?"

"Can't complain gorgeous, can't complain."

Without asking, Rene walked up to the cocaine pile on the coffee table and started chopping lines. He did four in a row before even uttering a word, like second nature. Jean-Michel, who could only admire the presumptuousness of the wretched queen, walked over to join Rene in the excess.

"You want to smoke some of the rock?" Jean-Michel asked the queen. Stephen was preparing the supplies in the middle of the room, the open space in which Jean-Michel filtered the symbols and language of civilizational ghosts into his painting. It was already 3pm, and they had only three hours to get these paintings over to Annina.

"Oh, baby, you don't have to ask me twice!" exclaimed Rene.

Jean-Michel packed the crack pipe and handed it to Rene. "Guest of honor, baby!"

"Oh, you most truly are a Radiant Child!" Rene giggled. He put the butane lighter to the clear pipe, caked in the resin of bygone hits, and inhaled a heaving cloud of cocaine fumes.

He exhaled... "By god, baby! Isn't it just fabulous! My mouth is simply not there, I can't feel anything in my face! It sounds like Max Roach is playing a solo in my ear! I'll never get sick of this."

Jean-Michel laughed hysterically. Although he liked to dance and he loved to party, Jean-Michel was typically morose and ill-humored. But Rene always made him laugh. "You crazy sunavabitch!" Jean-Michel took a hit himself.

"Well, how about a sneak preview of the paintings?" asked Rene.

"Step into my office, you old fag," said Jean-Michel. Before getting up, he did another bump of heroin to settle the crack and soothe his stomach, which felt squeamish. The last thing Jean-Michel could afford tonight was a case of diarrhea, so heroin would have to be his lifeline.

"You're going to kill your talent with that brown shit, Jean," said Rene. "It'll zap you of your creative vitality."

"Shut up, Rene. You want a sniff?"

"Fine," Rene said with a half grin, and he sniffed the bump of heroin off of Jean-Michel's elegant back hand.

They walked to Stephen, and Rene was transfixed by what he saw on the floor. His eyelids gaped open wide and his pupils dilated as they fixed upon the canvases. Jean-Michel always got a rush of libidinal pleasure when he saw someone respond to his art in such a pure way.

"My god, you gorgeous black boy!" said Rene, on his knees and pouring over every detail of the canvases, "These are magnificent!"

"I think they're all right," said Jean-Michel, blowing smoke rings around the apartment."

All right? I could fucking jerk off to these paintings you coy fuck!" said Rene, leaning over but looking backwards, eyes locked with the Radiant Child. "You're a fucking *genius!*" Jean-Michel just nodded, atypically humbled.

The three paintings that still needed to be brought to the gallery to be hung were three of what Jean-Michel considered to be amongst his best pieces. Maybe the only reason he hadn't signed them was that he didn't want that cow Annina to auction them off. With every painting sold, a piece of Jean-Michel's soul was being offered to the highest bidder. He knew this was a paranoid delusion but could not shake the feeling. He didn't know if it was the drugs or the reality of his position that made him feel this way.

In *Arroz con Pollo*, a dark-skinned male figure offers a woman a plate of chicken, while she appears to hold out her breast in reciprocity. Looking at it, Jean-Michel realized he identified stronger with the woman, who he shaded in blue. She was radiant. There was something about his relationship with sex in this painting. He'd always craved drugs, and recently heroin, more than he ever craved sex. He liked sex, but he was sure he'd have less of it if it hadn't become such a point of intrigue in the way that people fetishized him and his role within "the culture." He knew, on some level, he was selling his sex to get that chicken. Jean-Michel could only look at the painting when he was on dope, otherwise it all felt too *real*.

Per Capita made use of the crown logo that Jean-Michel had pioneered as SAMO, the graffiti slogans that, along with his now mostly former friend Al Diaz, Jean-Michel had drawn all over the city in ink and markers. Al was put off by Jean-Michel's success and Jean-Michel had no time or patience for Al's territorial pissings. Al was small-minded. Rigid. His contempt for Jean-Michel was so clearly rooted in his jealousy over what Jean-Michel had inside of him. Al lacked Jean-Michel's transcendent ambition. He didn't radiate. All of the shit talking he did about Jean-Michel's whoring and drug use was pure projection. Jean-Michel could fill his veins up with dope and fuck until his dick fell off and he'd still rise to heights that Al could never dream of, and they both knew it. The collapse of their creative partnership meant also the break-up of their band, Gray. Without these bedrocks, their friendship eroded fast. Jean-Michel had no intention of ever being a graffiti artist. He was a poet and a painter. He simply envisioned SAMO as a means of putting his stamp on the city. With his words reverberating throughout the minds of New Yorkers, his power would grow. And it did. *Per Capita* was stamped with Jean-Michel's free associative poetry.

"El Pluribus," it reads.

Jean-Michel used the collaging of texts to construct a hypnotic loop through which the meanings of American history would congeal and erase their own significations. Or something. Jean-Michel wasn't always sure what he was doing, but he knew it was good. It *felt* good. Depicted in the center of the piece was a black boxer carrying a torch; a touch of self-mythologizing. When people asked Jean-Michel where these images and these words came from, he seldom knew how to answer. They came from everywhere. They came from the infinite cosmos that existed within his psyche as it collected and processed information from the world exterior to it. Jean-Michel's mind was an antenna that collected the disorienting frequencies of the world during the information age: the city, art history, the television, world history, literature, poetry, the images of outsider art, the images of African art, ghosts, demons, spirits that sought to be reborn! Receiving, interpreting, processing, and outpouring information in his paintings, Jean-Michel's subjectivity was a black hole between two realities. Cannabis kept his mind open. Cocaine kept his mind sharp and buzzing. And, more and more, heroin kept him rooted in the real world, for he knew that if he climbed too far outside physical reality, he would never come back.

Greatness. To be great, no one, and I mean almost fucking no one can know what that's like. Al sure as fuck doesn't, Annina will never know that feeling. Damn, not even Rene here, crazy crack fiend queer, will know it. But I have it. I've always felt it, it runs through my veins and fills me up with warmth just like the oozing glow of the junk that I shoot. Because I'm great, I live by a different set of rules. No rules, no rules can be imposed on me and I will not follow them. I'm going to fly high and look at all these people from above and see them as the ants that they are.

Jean-Michel instructed Stephen to add some black paint to reinforce the texts on the paintings and asked that he apply his signatures. He was feeling jumpy and wanted to get out of the house. He sat back at the couch to prepare one more shot before going out for the night. While cooking up, he noticed Rene particularly seduced by the final painting, *Peso Neto*, which depicted a number of primitive heads, some emblazoned with the crown logo.

"You like that one, Rene?"

"Yes, Jean, it's… transcendent."

194

"It's yours, man." As he spoke, he pushed the needle in his vein, biting and letting the belt loose while the dope mixed with his blood. The shot felt particularly good. Jean-Michel was now in the void. Free. Radiant.

"It's yours, man." Jean-Michel had "given" Rene several paintings in the past already, only to end up passing them to his bloodthirsty dealer to be sold. He almost enjoyed disappointing this poof poet at this point. Rene was truly someone that he could hurt repeatedly and never alienate. Maybe true friendship is nothing more than the endurance of cruelty. At least, Jean-Michel liked to think of it as such.

"I'm not going to hold my breath this time."

Jean-Michel smiled. He had to get out of the house. He had to rule the city. "Hey Stephen man, I can't bring these paintings over to Annina, they look good. Just get them over there for me, will you?" instructed Jean-Michel to his assistant.

"Um, Jean, there are three of them, how am I supposed to do that alone?"

"Here man, here's a grand. Figure it out." Jean took $1000 out of his trousers' back pocket and threw it on the coffee table. Stephen was satisfied with the bonus.

"Come on Rene, let's go find some people before we head to the show."

Ever eager for the friendship of the Radiant Child, Rene replied, "Splendid," and took another hit of crack.

Jean-Michel and Rene headed out into the streets of downtown New York. The air was cool and the sun intensely bright. They looked like children walking down the sidewalk together; laughing, running and then stopping to walk once more, taking turns doing bumps from Jean-Michel's sack of cocaine. Jean-Michel felt overwhelmed by a sense of freedom. Like death didn't matter because he was unconstrained. He could do anything he wanted right now. What else would there be to achieve?

"Where should we go, gorgeous? We got some time to kill," asked Rene.

"Let's head to John's place, I heard some people are gonna be there," replied Jean-Michel.

"The devilish Lounge Lizard himself, splendid idea gorgeous, let's head there!"

They walked north up 3rd Ave. and took a right on 14th St. 14th was lined with the decadence of an American city. Pimps. Whores. Hustlers. Junkies. They were all out, giving the city its noble character. John Lurie was getting fed up with Jean-Michel's egomaniacal self-involvement. This, of course, only made Jean-Michel want to enrage him more.

Jean-Michel rang the buzzer.

"Hello," said Lurie in his thick, masculine, New York accent.

"What's up, bitch?" said Jean-Michel.

"Oh... Hey Jean." John's voice was tinged with resignation. He buzzed Jean-Michel and Rene in.

Walking in the apartment, there were far fewer people over John's than Jean-Michel had hoped for. Only John and Vincent Gallo, Jean-Michel's friend and former bandmate, both sitting at the kitchen table at the back of the minuscule studio apartment. John was dressed in a white, pin-striped shirt with the sleeves rolled up and a skinny tie. His cheeks were even more sharp than usual; he looked nothing short of glamorous (he was at the early stages of drug use, when the drugs actually made you look good). Vincent, whose face was a strange hybrid of bug-eyed features and boyish masculinity, seemed to define the very essence of "attractive ugliness." Rene and Jean-Michel walked forward to greet the two men.

Vincent got up and walked towards Jean-Michel, pulling him in for a hug. "So good to see you, you black bastard!" Jean-Michel always respected him for not walking on eggshells around his blackness. Vincent kissed him on the cheek. "I'm so proud of you!" Vincent expected nothing of anyone. In the past, this made Jean-Michel feel comforted. But now, lost in the grandiosity of his success, it made him a little bitter. He wasn't your average negro, and he didn't want to be treated like just another friend.

John didn't get up. He just nodded and motioned over to the kitchen table.

"Sit down, guys."

With everyone sitting around the table, Jean-Michel brought the baggie of coke out of his jacket pocket, and flicked it with his pointer finger, trying to inspire enthusiasm for the drug amongst his company.

"You boys want?" asked Jean-Michel. Everyone nodded approvingly. Jean-Michel started chopping up lines, which they inhaled through one of the many $100 bills he had in his pocket. He couldn't help but notice that John was even quieter than usual, chain smoking his Marlboro Reds and scowling. It was uncomfortable. Jean-Michel knew that John held contempt for him, but contempt he could handle (he even relished it in a weird way). But being ignored? That he could not abide.

"What's up John?"

John sighed, inhaling a massive cloud of tobacco smoke. He'd clearly been trying to avoid this conversation. "Do you even remember being here this morning?"

"Me? I was here?" Jean-Michel lied. He had cloudy memories of being at John's apartment early this morning, having walked over in despair and a haze of cocaine, heroin, and alcohol.

"I was scared, you fucking asshole. You looked horrible. Your nose was bloody. You were crying. If you are that afraid of your father, why don't you just cut him out of your life? I don't talk to my dad, I'm fine."

The anxiety that Jean-Michel had been repressing all day broke through his junk-constructed walls of apathy and overwhelmed him. He was absolutely terrified of seeing his father tonight, who had suddenly become "oh-so-interested" in his son's artistic career now that he was making more money than he ever did.

You evil motherfucker I know what you're doing, I see you, you old son of a bitch! You thought I was nothing but it turns out I'm not nothing — I'm everything! I'm everything that you aren't! I shoot this shit to kill the parts of me that are you, it's the worst parts! But I'm extra-human baby, you are oh-so-human. You're just a man, you're fuckin' small! I'm so big that you you're a bug, a bug that I could swat and kill at a moment's notice. Oh, you proud of me now? You're proud of yourself! You're proud because you think those ass beatings you gave me set me on the straight and narrow! Hah, I'll probably be dead before I'm 30! I hope you'd feel guilt, but I know you won't! I know you won't, because I won't.

Jean-Michel, seething at John's willingness to put his daddy issues on display in front of his friends, stood up from his seat. He didn't even look at John before motioning to Rene. "Rene, you ready? Let's head to the gallery."

The two men walked south to SoHo in silence. Jean-Michel felt slightly nervous that his show would be a failure, but the feeling passed quickly. He already knew in his heart of hearts that it would be a sell-out. His walk turned into a gallop, while Rene followed suit.

The gallery on 100 Prince Street was so mobbed with people that a fire would have surely resulted in nearly all of their deaths. Jean Michel felt giddy at the thought, he enjoyed the idea that he was so great they'd burn to death to stand before his genius. Rene put his right arm around Jean-Michel's neck, and pulled him tight,

kissing him on the forehead. "You beautiful black slut! You did it!!"
They laughed deliriously, bumping some more cocaine on a key.

When Jean Michel emerged through the gallery doors, a rip-roaring
round of applause broke out. Basking in the adoration of a crowd
of art world hanger-ons, reality collapsed upon itself. It felt like a
dream. Yet, so many friends among them. Glenn O'Brien. Diego
Cortez. Keith Haring. Anya Phillips. Paige Powell. Fab 5. They
were all there, they were all so proud of him. Suzanne was in the
crowd, and though she wouldn't look at him, he knew she was proud.
Even Andy Warhol was there, admiring *Arroz con Pollo* (apparently
Stephen had made it in time for the hang). But he didn't just want
Warhol's respect. He didn't just want his friends' pride. He wanted
their worship. And shockingly, he was getting it. Annina came
up to Jean-Michel to tell him that all the paintings had sold out.

"Cool," he said, dismissing her, even though he was happy to hear
the news. He just had no time for the old bitch.

Shortly thereafter, his father found him. He shook his hand,
employing the empty gesture of a distant father towards his
contemptuous son. "Son, this is wonderful, I can't believe it. My
son, a famous artist."

"Thanks pop, cool." To provoke him, Jean-Michel took a key
bump as he walked away from him, in plain sight. His father's
expression of silent disappointment was a divine gift. He couldn't
hurt him anymore. He signaled with his hands, pointing to the
back of the gallery, for his inner circle of friends to meet him
in the back. Once there, he emptied the entirety of the three
grams of cocaine that he had left onto Annina's desk. He put

200

on a tape he carried in his pocket. Sly Stone's *There's a Riot Goin'
On*. He snorted lines with his friends and felt so free! He felt like
the king of the world! He danced, and he danced some more!

As the party started to wind down, Jean-Michel felt an emptiness
wash over him. He was trying to scrape the remnants of the coke
into a cohesive bump, but it was mostly dust. He felt jittery and his
nose was jammed closed; he was mouth breathing as a result of the
blood and coke resin blocking his nasal passages. Without motioning
towards his chatty, coked out friends, he grabbed a slim brunette
in a leather rocker jacket who had been eyeballing him throughout
the night. Not the prettiest girl he'd ever seen but cute enough. He
looked in her eyes, smiled, and took her by the hand. He walked her
outside. In the alley next to the gallery, they kissed. She told Jean-
Michel that her mouth was numb. She asked him if he had any
coke. He smirked and shook his head. She grabbed him by the cock
and unzipped his pants, dropping to her knees. If his cock smelled
as bad as Rene said it did, she didn't seem to mind. The girl put it
all the way in her mouth down to her tonsils, and she sucked. She
sucked him for a long time. Jean-Michel was coming down from the
coke and could barely pay attention to her. After a while, she finally
asked, "is there something wrong?" Jean-Michel wasn't hard. The
coke and the heroin had robbed him of his vitality but he felt no
shame. She was, after all, just a gallery bitch. He put his cock back
in his pants and left her there, on her knees, without saying a word.

Jean-Michel went back to the gallery, and walked to the bathroom,
locking the door behind him. He removed his Armani jacket,
grabbed his remaining packet of heroin from its pocket. He sat
on the toilet and cooked another shot. His mind was cloudy, but
perturbed. Shouldn't a great man feel infallible? Why, Jean-Michel

thought, did he always feel like it was never enough? He injected the heroin, and his eyes rolled into the back of his head. He leaned back and dissolved into the complexities of his thought.

How long can this go on? Why can't a king find some relief? Who will kill me first? The CIA? The FBI? The art world? Or my fucking self? Why can't I be alone with what I have? Maybe death is the only real beauty. Perfect black. Perfect quietude. How much longer do I have? Do I want more than what I'll get? Oh, baby. They're bugging my phone lines, they're all after me and I can't quit because I don't know how but I want to quit and I'm tired. I'm tired of radiating. How old am I? I feel ancient? I'm positive I'm a soul who has lived 1000 lives. 1000 lives of suffering all to be great just once! I am the product of a spiritual evolution across space and time and now I'm exhausted from it all. Will the needle kill me? I hope not now, but maybe sometime soon…

Suddenly, someone knocked on the bathroom door. "Jean, are you ok gorgeous? It was Rene. "You've been in here a long time, babe, there's a dinner that we're supposed to attend."

Jean-Michel snapped back into reality, slapping his face back into its immediate surroundings. "Yeah, I'm good," he said. "I'll be right back out."

We are that radiant child and have constructed our lives to protect that little baby, constructing an adult around it to protect it from the unlisted signals of forces that we have no control over. We are that little baby, and that radiant child, and our name, what we are to become, is outside us, and we must become "Jean-Michel" - **Rene Ricard**

To radiate is to burn out quickly, is it not?

• epidemic/pandemic •

I graduated from Sandwich High in 2006, in a town within the Northeastern vacation destination of Cape Cod. Cape Cod is no longer famous solely for its seafood, beaches, and polo shirted WASP vacation setters, but for being ground zero for the worst ravages of the opioid epidemic. It's hardly unique for teenagers to experiment with drugs. Alas, there is – I believe, a healthier trajectory of experimental drug use than the one my Cape Cod friends and I embarked on. Maybe during earlier, groovier times, our boomer parents would have smoked pot, tried mushrooms or LSD, then got to college, snorted cocaine and popped diet pills for those exams. Hard drugs like opiates were most likely not a part of this journey. Heroin is a drug for the hardcore drug user, not for the kid looking to mess around a bit with illicit substances. But when I was in high school we smoked pot and then moved to OxyContin. By that point, OxyContin had been made widely available due to what are now universally accepted as the illegal practices of its manufacturer Purdue Pharma and money hungry, unethical physicians. As I'm writing this, liberals are on their social media pages celebrating the scientific advancements of companies like Johnson & Johnson for their rushed Covid vaccine. All the while, that same company is handing out $572 million for its aggressive marketing of opioid drugs. The villains of the true crisis are made into heroes of an arguably overblown and manufactured one.

During my teens, opiates were everywhere. As a result, my friends and I skipped the generally innocuous stages of experimentation and went right for the hard drugs, hardly even understanding what these pills were. It was now as normal to snort a highly addictive painkiller at 16-years-old as it was to eat mushrooms to appreciate nature and listen to music. In this cultural climate, opiate addiction was integrated into the cultural narrative of American youth itself. My childhood friends have died. Others have survived, but still struggle. I have mostly escaped the clutches of the opiate addictive loop, but to say that I'm totally free of the chemical (or, should I say, family of chemicals) would be a lie. I think about opiates every day. I dream about them often at night. And if a situation of relapse presented itself, I am not positive that saying "no" will be an easy feat. The poppy is a parasite, its allure cancerous. Even when benign, it threatens to metastasize once more.

Seven years after my rehabilitation, my relationship with opiates remains complicated. It's been years since I've used these drugs, and yet I miss the clarity I felt using them. During the process of writing this book and communing with the ghosts of dead junkie artists, I dreamed of using them once more. When I entered recovery for the second and last time in 2013, these recurring drug dreams haunted and tortured me. Professionals would say that such dreams are the manifestation of a subconscious lingering desire. A cosmic joke, with the inescapability of need as its punchline.

In one of these dreams, I find myself in a desert; the most barren wasteland my subconscious could ever project. I'll be walking along lost until stumbling upon a crater in the earth. Or, a pool, maybe. And in that pool, there'd lie a near limitless supply of 30-mg Percocet. I'd awake from the dream with a feeling of triumph, only to realize I was still a deeply stuck 26-year-old trying to stay clean. In an even more intense dream I'd inject heroin, but it was a variant with a never-ending effect. One shot would keep you in the bliss of junk for life. I could even feel the heroin flowing through my central nervous system. Paradise. Nirvana. And then I'd awake.

To my distress, these dreams returned for the first time in years as I was writing this book. I realize that the desire to feel junk would never completely leave me. Maybe that's fine. Maybe that's one of life's paradoxes — to know its most extreme pleasures and to know you can never experience them again. I've gotten used to it. But the discomfort and longing persists.

Oddly enough, one of my primary associations with opiate use is my severe allergy to cats. The first time I recreationally used hard opiate drugs, I was in this backyard barn owned by the parents of a high school friend. They were old school, Jack Kerouac reading, boomer hippies. Nice enough people, though I lost touch with that friend decades ago. The hippie friend wasn't a user but another friend present assured me of the exquisite high of OxyContin (in obviously less refined language). I was incredibly skeptical of trying this thing everyone kept talking about. I didn't like the idea of using a prescription painkiller marketed by the pharmaceutical industry. I had a romantic notion of drugs. The drug user as the outsider. The artist. Even at 16 years old, snorting painkillers seemed decidedly unromantic and vulgar. On this night, I relented.

There were cats in this barn. They caused me to persistently sneeze and left my eyes itching and watering. I often wonder if this had anything to do with my choice to walk out to the car and use for the first time. In that car parked on the lawn (the house itself was tucked into the woods and surrounded by vegetation), my friend introduced me to the OxyContin process. He took an 80mg tablet and put it in his mouth, sucking off the famous blue time release coating. Beneath the coating was a white pill — remarkably small as, unlike so many other painkillers, OxyContin is not bulked out with over-the-counter analgesics like acetaminophen or ibuprofen — that he placed on top of a woman's makeup mirror. He took a dollar bill and placed it over the pill, and then used his razr cell phone to crush it into powder. Once complete, he used a debit card to scrape the powder onto the mirror and chopped it into two lines, 40mg each (much too large a dose for a first time user, mind you). After sniffing the line, I remember the drip was far more pleasant than the chemically numbing effect of cocaine. Its flavor was like some artificial chalky blueberry, oddly consistent with the color of its coating.

While not exactly immediate, its effects kicked in rather quickly. A glorious warmth and comfort ran down my spine, and a pleasant nausea in my stomach spread outwards. The entire body glowed, now free of pain or tension of any kind. When I left the car, I puked. But, surprisingly, not even the puking felt unpleasant. Hiding my drug use from the rest of the crowd inside, I took one bong rip in the barn. After topping the pill off with cannabis, I couldn't keep my head up. I was lost in a paradise of my own consciousness.

An intense opioid high, experienced only before excessive use has built tolerance, is a peculiar experience. One cannot describe it as anything remotely psychedelic. It yields no insights, visions, or synesthesia. But its potent analgesic effect does produce a new awareness of the world. The night of my first OxyContin use, I could not sleep. I rolled around on my bed in my family home, restless but not totally awake either. And you don't bemoan insomnia, for the experience is beautiful. It is only during these first times that I experienced anything resembling the divine intoxication of the poppy as described by the Romantics. Byron, de Quincey and Coleridge, all related to opium as an ideal that has collapsed and vanished from the world we live in. Coleridge famously describes the dose of opium that sent him into a dream that he would never fully remember.

When I placed my head on my pillow, I did not sleep, nor could I be said to think…My imagination, unbidden, possessed and guided me, gifting the successive images that arose in my mind with a vividness far beyond the usual bounds of reverie.

It is stories such as Coleridge's which underlie a lot of our clichéd ideas around opiates and art. And yet, these stories and the experiences they describe somehow ring true. Because the first usage of any opiate — and I truly mean any opiate drug, heroin, Oxycontin or Codeine; the qualitative differences between these substances dissipate once you've used all of them at psychoactive dosages — is perfect. There's no better adjective to describe it. It's a state of perfection, of complete inner quietude. After snorting that first OxyContin, I spent 10 hours in bed. On my little bedroom entertainment system (TV, stereo, DVD player), I watched *Twin Peaks* and listened to Aphex Twin, the Butthole Surfers, and Wu Tang Clan. I found new beauty in it all. All the teenage angst that normally suffocated me, faded. It's not that my memories or pain were gone, exactly – I could still see the things about myself that bothered me. I still remembered all the things I'd done and felt guilty about. And yet, the negative associations of the memories felt so fucking unimportant. I could face all my guilt, all my traumatic memories, and stare them in the eye and smile. I was untouchable, cloaked in beauty, safety and warmth. To this day, thinking about that first time sends chills down my spine and waters my mouth. In *Kubla Khan*, Coleridge describes his personal nirvana – the Xanadu that he'd been reading about upon the ingestion of the divine opium:

> *In Xanadu did Kubla Khan*
> *A stately pleasure-dome decree:*
> *Where Alph, the sacred river, ran*
> *Through caverns measureless to man*
> *Down to a sunless sea.*

I too experienced visions of paradise. And yet, it was a paradise more direct. I saw myself as a famous avant-garde musician, worshipped by beautiful, smart urban women. Or a winning prize fighter, equally celebrated for ferocity and grace. I saw myself as a man. I saw possibilities everywhere. This lack of direction which had been a constant source of anxiety so far, broke down and I truly believed that there was nothing bad that could ever happen to me. Everything, whatever it was, would make me happy, content, and proud to be alive. That's what OxyContin gave me for the very first time.

But this was only once. I never again experienced an opiate high so pure. Since that day, I would forever be trying to replicate what I felt that first time. Because the opium of Coleridge and de Quincey is not the heroin and OxyContin of the 21ˢᵗ century. Those poets, brilliant as they were, were aristocrats in an era prior to the chaotic changes of industrialization and well before the Information Age. They had time to drug, think, sleep, and dream. That's not to say they had life easy, nor that the societal changes they faced weren't overwhelming and exhausting. But they didn't have an information highway to contend with. They didn't have a sentient object warming their pockets, flickering light and buzzing with new information every minute maximizing their inescapable alienation, did they? We are never given so much space to breathe, are we? No, we are stressed, worried, and wired into a system from the moment that we are born. And heroin does not free us from this system. As Burroughs understood so well, it accentuates these systems, and tightens their grasp around us. There is no fucking escape, and the only respite that junk addiction offers is the sense of apathy that it engenders. But apathy is an illusion. Or, it's an avoidance. Just because we tell ourselves that something is not there, does not mean that it's not there. It's there all right. And – we're trapped in it. In the 21st Century, opiates are not a paradise. They're a coping mechanism.

OxyContin cost $80 for an 80mg pill when I was in high school. It was an extremely expensive (not to mention, dangerous) habit for a high school student who worked as a busboy on weekends to pick up. I'll probably never forgive myself for the amount of tips I spent trying to get my hands on that fucking pill during my last couple years in high school. The opiate addict's life is often divided into a pre and after-opioid use period; mine was no different. While not perfect, I was a decent, honest, and lovable young man before I tried that first pill. Since that day; lying, deceit and manipulation became essential to the justification of my behavior and constant lack of money. Soon enough, all sorts of new, humiliating and degrading problems started kicking in. Once, I got fired from a pizza parlor when the camera caught me taking a knife to the bathroom to crush the pill into powder. When confronted by my former employer about the incident, I responded first with rage. I went into a spastic fervor, throwing pizza ingredients on the walls. Then, I wept, in a bizarre and inappropriate display of vulnerability. Though I don't know if this is the case with everyone, opiates made me every bit as emotionally erratic at inopportune moments as they made me numb and vacant for the majority of the time.

In a sense, the pill's cost was a blessing in disguise. Had it been cheaper, I would have used more of it, at a greater frequency. At this price, however, there was just no way for me to afford enough to truly develop a physical dependency. Thus, I never experienced withdrawal symptoms in those early years. I longed for the drug, and thought about it endlessly, but never felt its physical sickness. That would come later.

I made the disastrous mistake of going to the University of Arizona for my undergraduate studies (much too far from home for an immature dope fiend with delusions of grandeur). At the time, I was drawn to the desert aesthetically (a morbid curiosity, really) and very interested in David Foster Wallace, who briefly taught there (it is, after all, one of the settings in *Infinite Jest*). Entirely unsure of what I'd be doing in life — though I assumed something in literature or art — I seemed to have little ambition beyond consuming as many drugs and drinking as much alcohol as was humanly possible, and getting laid. I wince and cringe when I look back on myself during that time; I see an insecure dilettante with false bravado, riddled with confusion about what to do with his life. Youth is massively overrated.

I wouldn't get my hands on opiates, however, until my second semester; a rich, good looking kid from Los Angeles was hawking OxyContin just one floor above me in the dorm. His price per pill, $35 for an 80mg tablet, was a bargain. What unfolded during that second semester is just so predictable, so boring. The tablets I used to savor back home would now be hawked up my nose in one line, sometimes two of them in two lines. I alienated all of the friends I made; my roommate took me for a degenerate freak (and he was right), and my best friend, also attending the university, lost his trust in and respect for me. This entire project is a pointless and futile attempt at exorcism.

During that time, I found myself in a brief yet disastrous relationship with what I remember as an absolutely stunning girl from Tucson, who I had no connection with beyond our love of opiates. Even worse, despite her beauty I couldn't sexually satisfy her. I was either in mild withdrawal, and would ejaculate immediately, or totally junked out, and thus incapable of maintaining an erection. My shame was so great that I started lying about our sex life to friends. These lies eventually made their way back to her and ended our relationship. Sexual impotence is a common side effect of opioid abuse. Why then, you ask, would anyone continuously get high, knowing these humiliating consequences? The answer itself lies within the presented paradox: junk is *that* fucking seductive.

It's quite strange when you start realizing that you're becoming physically dependent on a drug. It's subtler than you'd imagine, and at the same time, completely apparent. You know it's happening; you just start caring less and less about it until it's not... Mikhail Bulgakov chronicles this journey with beautiful clarity and brevity in his novella, *Morphine* (1925). In that story, the young Dr. Bromgard moves to a country town to build a local practice. There, he learns that an old colleague, Dr. Polyakov, has taken mortally ill. When Bromgard visits Polyakov, he finds a journal that reveals the

213

source of Polyakov's sickness: morphine. The journal chronicles Polyakov's first morphine injection; a necessary measure to deal with unbearable back pain (a story that we can certainly all relate to during the era of *Purdue Pharma*). Ecstatic about the drug's ability to cease "all unpleasant situations," he enters a harrowing spiral. The doctor understands that he's becoming a dope fiend — his nurse tells him as much and he hardly disagrees — but the severity of his affliction is just not registered with appropriate sincerity until it's too late. In withdrawal, he quarrels with the nurse before she gives in and administers the shot. He assures her (and himself) that breaking his addiction will be easier: "A little morphine habit isn't addiction, is it?" he asks. Yes. An opiate habit is almost always addiction, solely because the pleasure of its effects vastly outweighs the negative side effects of a habit. Until its ravages have swallowed you into the belly of a life that would have been utterly repulsive to your former self.

Professor Carl Hart is a neuroscientist at Columbia University. He claims to be an expert in the studies of the effects of psychoactive drugs on the human mind. But his real infamy has been earned in his near shocking advocacy for heroin as lifestyle medication. Hart has come out as a "regular heroin user" and even claims that its use has made him a better person. In one of the more obvious psychological operations in an era of very obvious psychological operations, Hart manages to attach a libertarian, personal responsibility, anything-goes kind of lifestyle and infuses it with the rhetorical signifiers of racial justice. That he has risen to prominence during a time in which the opioid epidemic is finally being examined in parts of the country as the *real pandemic* shouldn't surprise anyone with half a fucking brain.

In any case, the difference between Hart snorting heroin as a tenured professor at an Ivy League college, and a working man taking pills to relieve his back pain, is vast. Opiates are easier to get hooked on than just about anything, and I can't wait for the day 10 years from now when Hart is in the press telling us how wrong he was. It's difficult for me to understand what it was about myself that made me so susceptible to opiate addiction, or what makes anyone susceptible to it. I was, for the most part, a happy middle class child supported by loving parents, despite their faults. That's a better hand than most people are dealt, no question. I suppose my transition into adolescence was not as straightforward. I've always been prone to a crackling anxiety that lurked just beneath the surface. A sense of unease, perhaps.

My first serious bout of withdrawal happened towards the end of freshman year, when the pill guy had left campus and I ended up temporarily without a source. Before my supply dried up, I was still excelling academically. Life was pretty good until then; I was living with free room and board, and a gig at a sandwich shop that kept me in drug money. The moment I ran out of pills, everything crumbled. For the first time, I found myself truly sick. I missed three days of class, as I was up all night in my dorm, puking in the showers. Perhaps most tragically, I almost cleaned up during these days. If I had stuck it out a couple more, I would have been renewed.

Instead, I learned that some guys I vibed with — art adjacent guys, who listened to noise rock and watched David Lynch films — were using heroin. Given that I had spent my youth worshipping Cobain, Burroughs, and Lou Reed, it took me less than two minutes to decide to get in on the action. Before I knew it, I was in one of these friends' dorm rooms, where his roommate — a tall, stocky, ginger

215

with an off-putting sort of emo look and a Flock of Seagulls hairstyle — had been selling black tar junk to finance his own out of control habit. I bought about $60 worth of dope, and learned how to use the drugs. I had to place a piece of the smack over tin foil, light it from below with butane, and chase the fumes, with either a dollar bill or a hallowed out pen (the dealer, sketchy fucking weirdo that he was, had filled his desk drawer to the brim with these used tins, almost as if he was begging to be arrested). Upon exhaling the first hit, the sickness totally evaporated from my body. The perfection of that high was unforgettable. Almost immediately, I was itchy, warm, in a state of heavenly relaxation. I had so much energy, strength and inner peace that I ended up going for a 10 mile run. It was 2am.

I cannot deny that I was driven to opiates during an alienating and terrifying period in my life. And yet, it's impossible to avoid the fact that this was the period that would define me as an artist. My way of thinking and working were developed during a time of daily dragon chasing and eventually, mainlining. I spent the summer working at a restaurant on Cape Cod with every dime made wasted on pills to ward off the sickness. Its evil metastasized an almost spectral presence in my life. It loomed over everything, constantly threatening to manifest and destroy me. I was happy to get back to Tucson and immediately resumed my black tar regimen. It was dirt cheap and potent. I was using it with two rock n' roll art kids and one profoundly odd Columbia drop out. He introduced me to the needle. My tolerance was so high already that I doubted I'd get that cinematic, eyes-rolling-into-the-back-of-my-skull high from tapping the mainline. The appeal of intravenous drug use was immediately evident. The effect was instantaneous; an indescribable inner calm and physical bliss that washes over you with a mesmeric power. Beyond its superior physical effects, I was also seduced by the protocol of mainlining. It was like holding a private séance: a deeply personal ritual involving flame, metal objects, sharp tools, and a mystical substance.

And for roughly three to four months, I injected black tar heroin every day. In what will, dear reader, perhaps be disappointing for you to know, my life as a severe heroin addict did not have the glamorous allure of *Trainspotting*. I did not have a group of friends wearing fabulous acid punk outfits who listened to Iggy Pop and Underworld with me as we committed petty crimes to support our habit. As a petit-bourgeois college student, I didn't have much heroin using friends at all, and when I did use with others it was often in a room full of Cape Cod lowlife wiggers that had very little interest in anything other than drugs and posturing as hard men. No, this period of junk abuse was predominantly spent alone.

But it was a creative period. Heroin and opiates shield you from distractions. Your exterior world becomes incredibly strict and tight: wake up, score, use. That is truly the only meaningful cycle. Casting all my university work aside, I became submerged into an endless search for new stimuli; noise music, transgressive fiction, cult cinema, true crime, pornography. I listened to records. To this day, Pink Reason's *Cleaning the Mirror*, Burial's *Untrue*, Royal Trux's *Twin Infinitives*, Portal's *Seepia*, or Nurse with Wound's *Huffin Rag' Blues* can send my body into a state of synthetic well-being OR unnerving sickness. I devoured literature: Burroughs, Norman Mailer, Peter Sotos, Dennis Cooper, Pynchon. I made collages and wrote poetry. From these private fascinations, buried in my narcotized subjectivity, emerged a creative practice. This, however uncomfortable, is the truth: I probably needed this strange, dark period of my life to unleash an artistic subjectivity. And as depressing as this point of my life got — and there is no way to minimize how repulsive I became to myself and others — I am still unable to completely write it off as a mistake. I clearly wouldn't be writing this book if I didn't go through it, and I doubt I'd be any kind of artist at all.

Eventually, my father discovered the ludicrous amount of ATM withdrawals I was making. It didn't take him long to realize that his son was a drug addict. He flew out to Tucson and got me into a methadone clinic. The methadone clinic is a humiliating, dehumanizing, drawn out experience in which you are brainwashed into needing more and more methadone and made into a subservient, docile subject to healthcare professionals who are trained to care far less about your health than the copious amounts of cash that your addiction earns them. You have to go there daily and stand in line with an assortment of shady individuals until you approach the counter and are given a cup of sickly, clear (or colored) fluid that you gulp down in front of the nurse. I remember an aging punk with bleach blonde hair who wore a leather jacket in desert heat that had tract marks and necrosis all over his hands. I remember an elderly man trying to get off painkillers accompanied by his ever culture shocked wife. I remember the young white trash guy in a wife beater who once brought a handgun to the clinic that was tucked into his back belt buckle. And just as I remember them, I'm sure many of them remember me: the skinny college hipster who thought he was too good to be there. But I wasn't better than any of them. No, I was one of them.

This goes on indefinitely until, predictably, the moment your insurance decides to stop paying the clinic's exorbitant costs. And then they cut you off. When that happened, I was finally forced to face the dreaded, prolonged withdrawal. I was up for five straight days and nights, medicating myself with marijuana and valium that barely touched the brutality of the sickness. I binged through the entire series of *NYPD Blue*; just seeing a picture of Dennis Franz on the internet brings a pulsating heat beneath the surface of my flesh until this very day. The logo of the show gives me diarrhea.

And, finally, on the sixth morning, I woke up. Refreshed. Restored. The feeling of non-synthetic health caused me to weep. I could feel my body. For the first time in over two years, it was absent need. This should have been the moment I swore drugs off forever and began to live my life as a healthy, functioning adult.

But I wasn't that. I was a narcissistic, self-involved piece of shit disconnected from anything but my pleasure principle. I wasn't prepared to deal with the social awkwardness, physical discomfort, and spiritual depletion that life after addiction entails. Heroin and opiates integrate themselves into your body and tend to become a second kind of blood. When they leave your system, you might be free of withdrawal, but you also feel *strange*. Your emotions grow uneven. You break down into tears at inappropriate moments. You find yourself lost in bizarre, murderous fantasies. You might, for instance, fantasize about killing your brother. And then, you might cry for entertaining such a thought.

My addiction was a period of crushing loneliness. When friends accepted me back into their lives after I cleaned myself up, I had forgotten how to act. I had forgotten how to relate to anyone. When I started dating again, it seemed like I no longer knew how talk to or connect with women. My return to sex was a disaster. I didn't have the heroin or the pills to slow down my circadian rhythms. When I did end up having sex, I found it near impossible to halt my ejaculation which always came a little too early. I was a chaotic mess of nerves and emotions. I started drinking again. Slowly, the regular partying reintegrated me into social circles. Which led to me doing cocaine again. And then...You get it.

By the time I moved to New York in 2011 to attend grad school, I had relapsed. Living in the East Village, I learned quickly how easy it was to get drugs in Manhattan. I met a dealer through Craigslist (yes, this actually used to be a thing). He was an excellent business man: respectful, disarming and punctual. He supplied me with a variety of opiate painkillers: morphine, Percocet, and OxyContin (at this point Oxy could not be snorted as Purdue Pharma had changed its formula under legal pressure). Only once did he ask to hide in my apartment for some time under the paranoid delusion that he was being followed. He had cocaine, and we chatted about our divergent paths for a couple hours until he felt safe to venture out in the streets once more.

Somewhere towards the middle of my first semester in grad school, he didn't have any pills on him. But he did have heroin. At that point, I was a daily user once again and saw no point in slowing down. I bought two grams of the junk and a set of clean spikes. My class schedule was light, so I was able to purchase drugs on my days off, while making sure I saw to all my academic work. Money felt like no issue. The junk was different from what I was used to. It wasn't black tar, but brown powder wrapped in individual packets emblazoned with various clever logos: the *Nike* swoosh, skull and bones, and otherwise. It had a different smell too. Black tar had the aroma of burnt hair while this brown powder was pleasantly sour once cooked. The dope was of a remarkably high quality, and I typically shot two bags at a time. For the first two months, every injection left me on the nod. I knew this behavior couldn't go on, and that I was risking both my education and my family's money (and grad school is already a waste of money). But I just could not stop. It was the most hooked I've ever gotten.

A year down the line, in the summer of 2012, I moved to Bushwick in Brooklyn. The now infamous neighborhood was at the beginning of its gentrification; split between its traditional working-class population and an influx of artists, students, and knowledge workers. For a while, it was both dangerous and exciting. Living with two friends (unaware of my heroin addiction), I would spend my days shooting junk and walking around, and my nights drinking, taking MDMA and cocaine, and dancing to techno music or nodding my head to noise. I kept my body "healthy" with an intense exercise regime in which I'd shoot smack before running and lifting weights, supplementing my caloric intake with protein shakes. While I remained in a pathetic state physically — somewhere between intense bouts of withdrawal and near-catatonic highs — I somehow, for the first time in my life, became sexually successful with women. It seemed that New York women were actually drawn to drug addicted wasters with delusions of future artistic greatness. My damage became a branding device. How ironic. It could have been a joyous time of my life.

Anna Kavan's *Ice* follows an unnamed protagonist searching for a woman across a brutally undifferentiated, frozen landscape. Under the ice, all experience is reduced to a dreary sameness: "Everything was misty and indistinct," writes Kavan. During that first year in New York, I did so much. I started making art, I made new friends, I fucked, I fought, I crossed the entire city. And yet – it was all covered in ice. When I attempt to recollect this time, my memory is flattened. Heroin abuse reduced everything into one extended moment. *Ice* isn't surreal, and neither is addiction. The surreal implies the intensification of subjective experience. Heroin addiction flattens it. Your life becomes a straight line, no matter what actually happens in it. There is no spiritual or emotional growth under the influence of junk. You are sick, alone, and incapable of getting out of bed. Or, you are out in the world feeling nothing. You don't process subjective experience as one normally does. Things happen, but they don't register as happening, like a key lever of your awareness has been stolen from you. Think of the first time you kiss a beautiful woman; under heroin, the fluttering in your chest that registers the excitement is gone. It's existence on auto-pilot. Highly depressing in the long-term.

This auto-pilot existence taints even the most extreme of scenarios. Towards the end of my days of junk, I was at a regular underground party called Ultra Velvet that transpired at a club on Broadway in Bushwick. Inside of the heavily mirrored club of Passion Lounge was trap music blaring from the speakers and an assortment of racially and sexually diverse "individualists" who were all desperate to one degree or another to have careers in the Hood by Air nexus of art, fashion, and clubbing. I hated the club, but went there from time to time. On one such evening, I showed up looking to restock on cocaine. I was on a lot of heroin and was having trouble staying awake on my short walk there. A zombie existence, animated merely by the need for more chemicals. I was approached by a dealer while nursing a Mai Tai at the bar. He was tall, big, black and assumedly gay, but not stereotypically feminine in any way. He was, in my mind, rather intimidating.

"You need any coke, molly."

222

"Just the coke, please."

The deal went down in the bathroom surrounded by gender-fluid "men" who were either too high to notice or care. After conducting the deal, the pusher left the bathroom and I proceeded to snort bumps off of my palm while sitting on a toilet in a stall. Rage pulsated over me when I realized the utter absence of lift that the "cocaine," gave me. It was either mostly or entirely baking soda. Furious, I set out to find the con man. My memories here drift in and out. I remember asking strangers throughout the crowd for the dealer, attempting to describe him in physical detail. Loose with my words due to the lack of self-consciousness afforded me by the heroin, I must have used rhetoric laced in either racial or sexual taboos, because I ended up on the floor. I came to sometime later in my bed, barely being able to turn on my side from my back with the bruises that lined my ribs and the welling on my jaw. Looking at my reflection in my iPhone camera, I was covered in blood. The dangerous life of the junkie that I was previously shielded from had become the life I was living. Something had to give.

Towards the end of grad school, I became convinced I would never be able to get off drugs. An incident on that Saturday night in September of 2013 spelled it out for me. Throughout the day, I had injected about 10 bags of junk (or, one "bundle"). Over-using the pulsating vein at the center of my left arm, I had one large tract park that was becoming really worrying to look at; having lost access to clean works, I was forced to re-use the same needles. Still, it felt like a glorious day. I was walking all around Brooklyn, stopping in at bars, and smoking joints before briefly returning home to shoot more dope. In the evening I went to a now defunct techno club called Output in Williamsburg, near the East River.

It was a fun place. Corny, but fun. There, I saw everything, from Merzbow to Richie Hawtin, and did jaw dropping amounts of drugs in its bathroom. Already under the influence of a gram of heroin, I smoked crack, snorted powder cocaine, did bumps of Ketamine, and was spiking my Heinekens with MDMA. I don't remember who performed that night. I don't remember dancing. I don't even really remember who I was there with, or even if I was there with anyone. I only remember the drugs. And I remember being in a cab, feeling like my heart was going to burst out of my chest as the stimulant drugs wearing off and the alcohol was taking over. I was covered in sweat and my head was pounding. I was scared. The world around me was glitching out, like the frequencies that construct our false reality were collapsing and through those holes I could see something like…. I don't know: "The real." There was so much confusion, and the sounds of the cab driver screaming at me enraged registered as a cacophonic, formless sound. I felt under threat, but couldn't decide who was after me or what there was to fear.

I remember getting out of the cab and dry heaving. The driver approached me. With concern? I don't know. I remember a confrontation. My body colliding into the other. But nothing beyond that is clear. I must have stumbled the rest of the short walk back to my apartment, unsure of what had just happened. When I got to my apartment, I tripped down the stair well into my basement bedroom. Having left the light on, I got a clear glimpse of my hands. They were covered in blood. My blood? Or the cab driver's? To this day, I'll never know. I don't want to know.

My body had to puke but my stomach contained nothing but liquid. In the stupor of the drugs I felt that another shot of heroin would settle things and calm me down. Maybe then, I could sleep. Reassess my life tomorrow with a clearer head.

I cooked a shot of three more bags of smack. I could barely walk or communicate, and yet still managed to mix the dope in the water with a junkie's precision. Before injecting, I put Throbbing Gristle's *20 Jazz Funk Greats* on. It must have been about 5 in the morning. I wrapped my Levi's belt around my right bicep (although the world was spinning around me, the ritual had become second nature by this point), tapped my forearm while tightening it, and finally found a juicy vein under my forearm, close to that large scar from an old drunken accident. I put the needle in, extracted the blood that would mix with the junk, and shot it back in. For a moment it felt like the best shot of smack I had ever had. It was as powerful and relieving as that first rush of OxyContin nine years prior. And then: BOOM!

I fell off my chair on the hard floor. I felt myself sinking, as if buried beneath the Earth and looking up. I was positive that I had just overdosed myself. I was suddenly aware of the situation at hand. I remember trying screaming but no words came out, like being buried alive. My roommates were out. There was no one who could save me. My will to live animated my whole psyche, and yet I was totally calm. If you could have seen me, you would have thought I was at peace. Yet within that quietude was total horror. My mind battling my body and begging it not to die. Me begging the God I never truly believed in not to let me die. So, I just lay there and tried not to fall asleep. Every time I nodded out, I would be jolted back into consciousness by the sheer fear of dying. I did not want to die. I never wanted to die, I thought, despite living at the edge of it. After some time passed, I realized that I was still alive. I was able to get back up and walked to my bathroom. I threw water on my face. "What the fuck am I doing?"

What followed was neither dramatic nor interesting. I checked myself into an outpatient clinic that wouldn't interfere with my studies. The doctor put me on a Suboxone program designed to gradually bring me off opiates. Over time, I came off them entirely. For a long time, I would never, ever discuss my years of addiction with anyone. Unlike so many of the junkie artists I loved, I was deeply ashamed to have lived like that. But why? Opiate addiction is the spiritual malaise and medical crisis of our era. We are arguably the first generation in history where junk addiction is no longer a signifier of outsideness, but one of commonality. Just last year over 81,000 more people died of opiate overdoses.

Heroin showed me the deepest recesses of my mind. I do not fear darkness nor sickness. There are times when I miss the clarity of junk, its glow, its warmth. But I would not trade this awareness for those ephemeral pleasures. Life after opiates feels heightened. This book was conceived as an excision of the tissues of the past. But the past is actually a limb, the severing of which would be fatal.

NINA POWER

◆ postface ◆

Drugs are, above all, a visceral contribution to the philosophy of time. Every culture has its own idea about how events should unfold, regardless of how things tumble out. In a culture dominated by an endless linearity, conceptions of 'progress', an endless 'always-on' mentality, a grasping relation to the future, it is no surprise that any attempt to jam a spanner in the works, to step outside of time (ecstasis), to claim a circle within a line, takes hold. Some are more open than others to these kinds of experiences, and some suffer the promise of the ouroboric more than others: those for whom the present is flat, those who understand the future as 'more of the same' or cannot wait for the current cycle to end.

Substances of all kinds have regretfully become desacralized, taken out of collective, ritual contexts. No longer tied to seasons, festivals, carnivals, we have instead an endless party where everything is available, but with no structure, no friends, and no meaning. Substances are rarely a gateway to contemplation, the divine, entheogenesis, but perform the function of a closed loop, a cave to hide in, while outside the mechanical universe whirrs away.

Drugs are not only time machines - they are also systems of ideas, refractions of the crystal. There is a paranoia induced by (some) drugs, but there is also the possibility of seeing the world, or the cosmos, differently. This cannot but include the *polis*, where men and women come to decide what the best way to live might be. Drugs have been and are being used as a weapon against populations. There is no doubt that some drugs suit particular regimes better, and that at different times what was once a gateway to subversive ideas becomes a mechanism of control. There is no doubt that some companies profit from the destruction of populations through the distribution of licit and illegal substances. Chemical social murder.

The insights occasionally afforded by chemically altering your baseline state sometimes come at the price of an altered relation to 'normality', particularly when this normality is quite openly and visibly insane. There is no going back. Drugs are not necessarily a slippery slope to 'harder' drugs, but rather to the possibility of contemplating more and more reality. This is how to have an expanded relation to truth, Nietzsche's perspectivalism: the crystal turns, the tree is chemical, mythic, poetic, natural, a part of everything else, somewhere for birds and squirrels to live and when chopped down, material for our own habitation. The tree is living and it is dead. To see even a single tree from multiple perspectives is to come alive in the light of the truth, that truth is *itself* multiple.

The outer world is transformed, but the inner one is too, often to the extent that the divisions of inner and the outer no longer make sense. Adam Lehrer's paean – of course an ambivalent one – is primarily, but not only, concerned with what drugs, and in particular, opiates, and at times even more in particular, heroin, can do, or not do, for art and artists. Let us not say that this book is about 'creativity', for even the most philistine will surely cringe at this word.

But rather we wend our way through a series of experimental imaginings, channelings and communing with the dead, or soon-to-be-dead, in their mediated junk-state. Lehrer's *Communions* is no moral handbook, either, for our world is too full of judgement. It's hard not to feel today that we are living through a certain kind of revenge against the creeping victory of the post-war absence of morality and the celebration of a hyper-individualistic hedonistic nihilism. We are now faced with the quite-possibly-worse horror of a post-Christian neo-morality in which people are deemed 'good' or 'bad' with no possibility of either being ambivalently flawed or being forgiven. A neo-feudal intra-human self-dividing along the lines of who gets to belong and who, as Frank J Miles puts it, gets to be vermin.

Every age has its drug. Lehrer writes 'during my teens, opiates were everywhere'. The poor get painkillers, the rich kids get uppers to treat their 'attention problems' and to ensure they produce an endless stream of work to ensure they get into the 'best' colleges and jobs, all the while pledging their allegiance to a politics of 'equality' to which their actual lives bear no relation, and never did. The opioid epidemic killed at least half-a-million Americans between 1999-2019. Big Pharma, the Sacklers in particular, squeal and twist to avoid responsibility. In any case, what does it matter? These were the kinds of 'deplorable' Americans who might have voted for Trump, who probably now refuse to get vaccinated. They weren't going ever to contribute to the great liberal culture of major US cities. They were never going to write an article that people on their laptops in coffee shops would read in order to check the correct position for the week. They live, and lived, in a kind of no-man's land.

Can we imagine an age to come when there will be a different relation to drugs? A re-ritualization? A return to collective inebriation in the name of something higher? It doesn't even have to be so far away – a particular moment in the calendar, a remembrance of place. Drugs that ramp up the chronic individualism of our age and then seemingly provide the answer in the form of warmth, confidence, expansiveness, and sociability play a cruel trick. A means to an end becomes an end in itself. Death beckons. Time is out of joint. To get out of the loop of desire seeks a new object: but, thrust back into the world, there is only what was there before. The trick – if there is one – is to reconfigure it. To see anew what before was only *boring*. The struggle to get back to what was always there is the passage from the underground to the sky, without the assistance of anything artificial. Refuse the easy option. Notice everything.

Does Lehrer seek to redeem the most narcotic of experiences by tethering it to artists, writers, actors and musicians? Nothing here is an unequivocal celebration. The subtle flip from mediating muse to full-on domineering compulsion is not inevitable, but it is always there as a possibility, and kicks in much sooner than you could imagine: 'It's difficult for me to understand what it was about myself that made me so susceptible to opiate addiction, or what makes anyone susceptible to it' writes Lehrer. This is the eternal mystery of the addict, even where there are external 'reasons' why substance abuse might 'make sense' – a shitty childhood, a traumatic experience or ten, a prescription for localized pain relief that starts to look like the solution to general existential suffering.

It is debatable whether an addict, once hooked, ever stops being an addict. The ubiquity of caffeine dependency, for example, is unremarkable, because millions of people live their whole lives without needing or wanting to give up tea or coffee or cola – yet if you do the withdrawal is punishing and life shudders as it does whenever something is taken away that has become a part of your neurophysiology. But other addictions are more oblique to the everyday. Hard drugs separate people from the others. Sometimes you have to cut out everyone you used to snort/inject/drink with, and sometimes they cut you out too. People are a kind of drug too, and as for music, images, moving or still, well, there is nothing more gripping, which is why humanity periodically undergoes bouts of iconoclasm, overcome by the extraordinary force of art.

If you have ever been addicted, particularly to something that has a major effect on character – alcohol, opioids, amphetamines – and you 'get clean', the world takes on an aspect of what can only be described as a 'sober trip'. The intoxicated frame does not ever go away. The times you were 10,000 feet above and 20,000 feet below remain as places you once knew. You remain there, imprinted on height like the shadow of an angel consisting entirely of energy. The things you thought you knew then you still know now, but you're standing at the bottom of the escalator. And what was it we knew the first time? Drunk, clambering up the stairs in my uncle's house at eleven I felt *free*. But what burdens was I carrying then for goodness sake? What need did I have to get 'out of my head'? There were techniques I could have learned, but I did not. The saturation, the warmth.

But this was only once. Lehrer notes the paradoxical innocence of the *first high*. The predisposition, the baseline mood: what would it be like to be someone else? Would someone else's life feel like an endless scream, or would it feel cozy? To feel the constitutive lack that we all have, the fissure, the howl that drives us to speak, that pushes us into separation: well, simply, do some feel it more than others? Go to any meeting for addicts and the only thing that unifies anyone is that they are there and alive and trying to stay off whatever it is that hooked them in the first place. There is no obvious 'tell'. No halo. No look. No specialness.

To even divide the world into addicts and non-addicts is a difficult, and unedifying task. Some imagine that they are addicts forever, that some switch has been incorporeally switched forever, some brain rivulet has been permanently diverted to respond in the worst possible way when the old thing floods in. Here there is no moderation, no way back, only the white-knuckle grasping hold of the light. For some, it's a phase, and when circumstances change, their desire does too. Who knows. Everyone, artist or otherwise, has to decide. Up or down. Life is too complicated to say simple things such as 'without X, I will no longer be an artist', though the romantic fantasy is always there: who am I without this? Can I still make work?

Adam's book is testament to the fact that the answer to this final question is always: yes, if you can make it. And those who do may not stand on the shoulders of giants, but they will sleep cradled in the arms of ghosts.

CPSIA information can be obtained
at www.ICGtesting.com
Printed in the USA
BVHW051220040822
643794BV00004B/61